Demon

in the

Mirror

SUNCOAST PARANORMAL 5

by

Lovelyn Bettison

This is a work of fiction. Names and incidents are products of the author's imagination. Any resemblance to actual persons living or dead is entirely coincidental.

Nebulous Mooch Publishing

2021

Prologue

Janet turned off the television and strained her ears, listening to the silence. Had she heard something, or was it just her mind playing tricks on her? She sat still, her arm outstretched, and finger poised over the red power button on the remote control. Cocking her head, she tilted her ear upward ever so slightly as if doing so would improve her hearing. Just when she'd convinced herself it was nothing, the sound happened again—a low thump directly overhead.

"Frank? Is that you?" she called into the still air, knowing there was no way her husband was upstairs. Frank lay sleeping in his hospital bed on the first floor, just yards away from her. She had checked on him a few minutes ago. He had been ill for months now and couldn't get out of bed on his own to use the bathroom, let alone climb the stairs.

Silence answered her, as she expected it would. Janet's arm began to ache, so she lowered the remote control into her lap without turning the television back on. Something was wrong. She could feel it. Then she heard the noise again followed by a slow creak.

Her stomach dropped. She swallowed hard and chewed on

the inside of her cheek. Maybe she had left the window open upstairs, and she was hearing the wind, but it was a hot windless night and that wasn't the noise wind made. Maybe an animal had gotten into her house. The Armstrongs next door had just had a problem with fruit rats in the attic.

She put the remote control on the coffee table and stood in the cramped living room. Her purse sat in the maroon velvet chair next to the sofa. She rifled through it and pulled out a can of pepper spray. Holding the spray, she took a deep breath and started toward the stairs.

The creaking sound happened again. Scree. Long and slow, it dragged through the air.

She jumped. Her heart rose into her throat. "It's nothing," she said to herself as she walked to the back hallway. Before going upstairs, she peeked into the room where Frank slept. He was painfully thin now, bones poking out at his shoulders. The skin across his face was pulled tight over his cheekbones. He lay with his face turned away from her, his mouth slightly open. She wished she could wake him and tell him she had heard a noise. Then he could go upstairs and take care of it. Those days were gone. She would have to take care of these things herself now. Eventually, he wouldn't be here at all. The thought made her heart ache.

Scree.

She looked toward the staircase. How she wished she had left the hall light on upstairs. Swallowing the lump in her throat, she held the pepper spray out in front of her. "Hello?" She climbed the stairs cautiously, her hands trembling. "Is somebody up here?"

No one answered.

When she got to the top⌐⌐⌐ of the stairs, she flipped on the hall switch, flooding the area in cold white light.

Scree.

The bathroom door stood open, swaying on its squeaky hinges. When she reached into the bathroom to turn on the light, her heart hammered in her chest as she imagined a hand reaching out and grabbing her arm.

Nothing happened.

The light over the sink flickered on. She looked behind the shower curtain.

No one.

She looked up to see the window next to the toilet open just a crack. Had she done that? She didn't remember opening it, but she had been so out of it recently that she couldn't say for sure she hadn't. She hurried over and pushed the window closed, making sure to lock it. She would check the other rooms in the house just to make sure, but she had found the source of her terrifying noise. She would oil the hinges in the morning. She knew Frank had some kind of spray oil he used for that kind of thing somewhere in the garage.

She took a deep breath and rolled her shoulders back, trying desperately to release the tension in her muscles. She walked through the bathroom past the mirror hanging over the sink. Out of the corner of her eye, she caught sight of a dark shadow in the mirror. It clouded the edge of her vision, but when she turned her head to look directly into the mirror, it was gone. Her own reflection stared back at her. Her face was round with plump cheeks that sagged slightly. Her gray hair was growing in, leaving an ashy strip close to her scalp. She'd have to get to the hairdresser and have it touched up to chestnut brown again. She leaned into the mirror to get a closer look at herself. Her complexion was sallow, and the new wrinkles in her forehead and between her eyebrows betrayed how much she worried these days.

An image flickered in the mirror over her own reflection. A slim man with a long narrow face stared at her, his mouth open in a scream.

For a moment, she felt disoriented. She nearly fell, but the cool plaster wall stopped her. When she looked at the mirror again, she only saw her own haggard expression. She blinked a few times. She was so tired her mind was playing tricks on her. She would go to bed early tonight. She promised herself that.

With the window locked firmly, she investigated the other rooms in the house. They were all empty as they should have been. She went down the stairs, still holding the pepper spray in her hand, but now it hung casually at her side. When she got to the bottom of the stairs, she looked in on Frank again. She was just about to step away from the door when he turned his head and looked at her with wide-open eyes.

"You're awake." She stepped into the room.

His chest rose and fell rapidly as if he were out of breath. She hurried to his bedside. "Are you okay?"

"I'm sorry." His voice was a rasp. "I didn't know what I was doing. I didn't mean to…" He shook his head. "I'm so sorry, Janet. You have to forgive me."

She looked at his worried face, and her heart melted. She reached out and touched his gaunt cheek. "I don't know what you're apologizing for, Frank, but whatever it is, it's okay."

He took in a wheezing breath. "No, it's not. It will never be okay again."

"What do you mean?"

His breathing slowed, and he got a faraway look in his eyes.

"Frank!" She gripped his shoulder.

His head lolled to the side, and his jaw went slack. Drool spilled over his lips onto his pajama shirt.

Panicked, Janet called an ambulance.

Chapter 1

Cheryl squeezed her eyes closed in an attempt to shut out the outside world, but she still couldn't shut out the music pumping through her mind. The incessant disco beat seemed to crowd her thoughts at the most inconvenient times. Her head pounded. She opened her eyes to see Adam and their new client, Janet, staring at her. They both looked concerned.

"Are you okay?" Adam asked. He walked over to her and put his hand on her arm as if steadying her.

She shook her head. "I just have a bit of a headache." She looked at Adam, hoping he would understand. She didn't want to tell a new client that a ghost had been harassing her with an annoying disco beat, and she'd been unable to concentrate on anything for what felt like weeks now. "I'm sorry." She looked at Janet, who had a friendly round face. "Continue with your story."

Janet cleared her throat and twisted around, glancing behind her as if checking to make sure no one else was listening. "It's hard to explain. To tell the truth, I feel like I'm a little batty." She looked at the floor before making eye contact with Cheryl again. "I've been seeing strange things around the house, but I can't really explain what they are because they always happen on the periphery of my vision. Maybe I'm imagining things. I'm not sure." She tucked a strand of dark brown hair behind her ear. "The bathroom mirror has really been freaking me out recently. I keep covering it up, but when I go in there, the sheet I put over it is gone."

"Why have you been covering the bathroom mirror?" Adam asked. He had let go of Cheryl's arm now and stood next to her with his hands casually in the pockets of his khaki pants.

"I think I saw something in it. I'm not sure. Every time it happens so fast that..." She shifted on her feet. "Do you know how they used to put frames of disturbing images into scary movies? Rumor has it they did that with The Exorcist back when they first showed it. That's why people were so terrified. Women fainted, and people had to get up and leave the theater. It was because they had inserted single frames of much more disturbing images than what you were seeing on screen into the movie. Your conscious mind doesn't pick up on it, but your subconscious does." She paused for a moment as if giving them time to digest what she had just said. "Well, that's kind of what has been happening to me, except it's not a movie; it's my real life. Every time I look in the mirror, I see flashes of something that isn't my reflection."

"What else are you seeing in the mirror?" Cheryl asked.

Janet pursed her lips and thought for a moment. "I'm not sure because it happens so quickly, but I think it's a man. He's scared, or he's trapped. I don't really know, but I do know that it terrifies me."

The music in Cheryl's head began to fade, and she was grateful for the relief. She couldn't have her client's story drowned out. Maybe now she would be able to sense something if there was actually paranormal activity in the house. She took a deep breath and looked around the crowded living room. It was packed full of dark wood furniture carved with intricate designs. Some of the pieces were quite nice, like the dark wood hutch that sat against the wall next to the front door. She liked the detailed carvings of flowers and vines trailing along its edges. There was too much furniture in the house for her taste though. "Are all of these antiques?" she asked, trailing her hand along the top of a solid-looking dresser.

"Yes." Janet smiled. "I just love old furniture. I can't stop buying it."

"Do you remember if the activity you describe happening in the house started after you bought an antique?" Cheryl asked.

Janet shook her head. "I haven't bought anything since Frank's been ill. Honestly, I don't have the extra money, and"—she gestured around the room with open palms—"I don't think I could fit anything else into this house. I should probably try to sell some of it." She let out an uncomfortable laugh. "My husband would love that. Too bad..." Her words trailed off.

Adam took a step toward her and reached out a tentative hand before pulling it back as if realizing he shouldn't be trying to physically comfort a stranger. "I'm so sorry about your husband's illness. Did this strange activity in the house start when he got sick?"

She thought for a moment. "Yes, I think so. It started about the time he started hospice care."

Adam nodded knowingly. "It's times like these when you are emotionally vulnerable, or you have chaos in your life that you are most susceptible to being haunted." Adam looked at Cheryl, who had begun to wander around the room looking at the various pieces of furniture. "Are you picking anything up?"

The way he asked the question made Cheryl laugh inside. Sometimes it was like she was an antenna searching for a certain radio frequency. She shook her head. "Are you?"

"Not yet." He turned his gaze back to Janet. "That doesn't necessarily mean there's nothing here. Sometimes it takes a few visits before any spirits will show themselves to us."

It all seemed so strange. When Cheryl had run away to Florida, she never imagined this would be how things would end up. She didn't really even believe in ghosts, let alone think she would be communicating with them and dating someone who could see into parallel worlds. Life had become so strange.

Janet's face flushed, and she turned her head to look behind her again. Cheryl wondered what she was checking. "I have been tired recently. Maybe this is all in my head." Her voice broke, and she raised her hand to her mouth.

"That's not what we're saying," Cheryl said. "Everything you're experiencing could be real. We just haven't seen it yet. That takes time, and we've only been in this room. Why don't we go upstairs to the bathroom and take a look at that mirror that's been giving you problems?"

Janet nodded her head, but her shoulders slumped. "Follow me." She turned and walked toward the hall behind her.

The thumping of the music in Cheryl's head stayed at an acceptable volume. It was quiet enough to be annoying but not so loud that it prevented her from working. She wished it would go away, but it had been relentless all day. She followed Janet through the living room to the back corridor with Adam close behind her. The staircase was off a small, dark hallway. To the left, the door to another room was open just a crack, and Cheryl caught sight of the hospital bed where Janet's husband lay resting. She could only see a sliver of the room—the top corner of the hospital bed and a bit of the spotted skin on his bald head. She fought the urge to reach her hand out and push the door open.

Noticing Cheryl looking into the room, Janet said, "He gave me a scare the other night, but it turned out to be nothing. He's up and down a lot these days, but mostly down."

Cheryl remained stopped in front of the door, looking into the room. "Have you noticed anything strange in his room?" She wanted so badly to go inside.

Janet started to speak but changed her mind. Then she shook her head. "Do you need to look inside?" Before Cheryl could answer, she walked over and pushed the door all the way open. "How is he doing?" she asked the nurse who sat on the sofa at the far side of the room, reading a paperback novel.

The woman wore navy blue scrubs. She looked up from her book, her face stern. "He's been sleeping." She glanced at Cheryl and then at Adam before returning her gaze to her book.

Cheryl looked over at the thin man lying in bed, snoring. His light blue pajamas were draped across his skeletal frame. A thin mint-colored blanket was pulled up to his shoulders. As she looked at him, she saw something behind him. A man so tall his head nearly touched the ceiling with long arms and a narrow face flickered into view for only a second before disappearing completely. Cheryl reached out and grabbed Adam's arm. "Did you see that?"

The nurse looked up from her book.

Janet looked at the nurse, her face tense. "Sorry to bother you, we were just checking in on Frank." She rushed Adam and Cheryl from the room.

"But I saw something in there. We need to check it out,"

Cheryl said as she was shoved through the door.

"What did you see?" the nurse called from her place on the sofa.

"Nothing," Janet replied over her shoulder as she rushed them from the room. She pulled the door closed and then leaned into Cheryl and Adam and whispered, "I haven't told anyone. I would much rather you didn't talk about this in front of the nurse or Frank."

Cheryl wrinkled her face. "I need to talk to as many people as possible to make sure we know what's going on. I saw something in that room. They both spend a lot of time in that room, so they might've experienced something too."

Janet shook her head emphatically. "I realize I might be losing my mind. I don't want anyone else to know. Frank is going through enough right now. He doesn't need the burden of worrying about what his crazy wife is doing." She spoke in a loud whisper. Determined, she walked past them to the stairs.

"If you really want us to help you, we need access to everything." Adam knew just as well as Cheryl that limiting who they talked to or what rooms they could investigate might make this case impossible to wrap up. Cheryl wondered if he was thinking what she was thinking. They might not even be able to help Janet.

"Follow me. I'll show you the bathroom." She started up the steps without looking behind her to make sure they were following her.

The music in Cheryl's head began to rise again. The thump-thump in her brain made her head ache. The music grew as if someone had turned up the volume to full. Cheryl stopped on the stairs and put her hand to her head. She closed her eyes again. When she opened them, Adam had stopped next to her and was looking at her. Janet was still walking up the stairs.

"Are you sure you're okay?" Adam asked.

This time Cheryl shook her head. "The music is so loud I can't even think straight. I think I might need to wait in the car. I'm starting to feel a bit sick."

"Janet," Adam called up the stairs.

Janet stopped suddenly and turned around.

"Cheryl's not feeling well and needs to wait in the car. I'm going to take her out there, and then I'll come back in to see the bathroom." He didn't wait for Janet to answer before taking Cheryl by the arm and leading her down the stairs.

"I'm sorry," Cheryl called to Janet.

Janet's face softened. "You don't have to sit in the hot car. You can wait in my living room."

Cheryl didn't want to wait in the cramped living room. She needed privacy in case she had another vision of the dance floor. The last thing she wanted was for them to come back downstairs and find her dancing in the living room. "That's okay. I'd rather wait outside." If her head wasn't hurting so much and the music wasn't playing so loudly, she might've tried to sneak another glance into the room where Janet's husband lay sick. But she wasn't feeling well enough for that, so she hurried past the door and walked with Adam outside.

"Are you sure you'll be okay out here?" he asked as he handed her the car keys.

"Yeah, I'll be fine." Her voice was weak, but that was all she could manage. "Just a few minutes alone in the car should help a lot." How she wished that was true. The problem was that no matter how much time passed, she didn't seem to be able to escape this. She needed to figure out what this ghost wanted so she could have her life back, but figuring that out was challenging when the ghost refused to talk to her. She'd have to make a better effort to communicate with him because she couldn't live with this music in her head forever.

***

"There it is." Janet nodded to the closed bathroom door. "I like to keep the door closed. It freaks me out a bit."

"Do you mind?" Adam motioned to the door.

"That's why we're here." She took a step back.

He turned the knob slowly, feeling a bit of trepidation himself. The door swung open to reveal a perfectly ordinary bathroom. A white sheet covered the mirror over the sink. He stepped inside. Humidity hung in the air, and the bathroom had a damp, earthy smell. Adam looked around hoping to feel something, but nothing in the room made his senses tingle. "You usually see something in the mirror?" He pointed at the ghostly white sheet.

Janet nodded. She still hadn't entered the room, but she cautiously stepped near the doorway. "Yes, that's where I saw it. He shows up quickly just for a split second. Long enough to scare me but not quite long enough to really register what he looks like."

Adam wondered if it was the same ghost Cheryl had seen in Frank's room. He wished she could be up here with him. He tugged the sheet, and it slid off the mirror and puddled into the sink. His reflection stared back at him. He stepped close to the mirror and leaned in, hoping to see the phenomenon Janet described. "How often do you see him?"

"I don't know. I've seen him a few times." She looked at Adam, and he noticed she refused to look at the reflection in the mirror. If she did, would she see something he couldn't?

"Does it happen right away, or do you have to be looking at your reflection for a long time?"

Janet laughed. "Do I look like someone who would be

looking at my reflection for a long time?"

Adam shrugged. "I'm just trying to find out what you see and when you see it." He looked back at his reflection and waited.

Janet remained in the doorway with her hands gripping the doorjamb.

"Where are you?" he whispered at his reflection.

Nothing happened.

Adam picked up the sheet and covered the mirror again. "I'm going to set up some cameras around the house to see if they pick up anything unusual."

Janet crossed her arms over her chest. "That's fine, but you can't set anything up in Frank's room. I don't want the nurses to think I'm spying on them."

Adam grimaced. "Since that's the room where Cheryl saw the ghost, it would be most useful for me to set the camera up in there." He really did want to help her, but she was making this difficult. "Can't you tell the nurses what's going on or make up something else as an excuse?"

She shook her head. "I'd rather not."

Aware of Cheryl waiting in the car, he decided not to argue with her about this point. "Okay. I'll get the cameras, then."

After all the equipment was set up, Adam got back into the car to find Cheryl sitting in the passenger seat with her head in her hands. "Is the music still going?"

She nodded but didn't bother to look up at him.

"Is there anything I can do?"

She uncovered her face and looked at him with frustration in her eyes. "Find out what this ghost wants from me."

"I wish I could." He started the car.

Her phone lit up in her lap. She ignored the call. "I wish they would stop bothering me." She put the phone in her purse and dropped it to the floor.

"Who?"

"Debt collectors, who else?" She frowned. "I didn't have the money yesterday so what makes them think I'm going to have it today or even tomorrow. I still don't have it." She shook her head as she spoke.

"I can help you out. If you need to borrow some money, I have some put away." He had made this offer before and already knew what she would say.

"Borrowing money from you is still borrowing money. That's what got me into this mess. I have to find a way out of it myself."

"But if you borrow it from me, you won't have to pay interest on it." Jules, Adam's sister, wouldn't approve of him even offering to help Cheryl pay off her debts. She always told him loaning money to a girlfriend would be a terrible mistake. He'd made this mistake before and never saw a dime back, but with Cheryl things were different. They were business partners, and he had a feeling their relationship would last a very long time. He would gladly settle her debts to help her live a better life.

She closed her eyes and leaned back in the seat. "My head hurts too much right now to think about money."

"Okay, but you don't have to suffer. I just want you to know the option is out there."

She opened her eyes and turned her head to look at him. "I know you're trying to help me out, and I appreciate that, but I have to learn how to stand on my own two feet." She parted her lips like she was about to say something but then pressed them together without speaking.

"What?"

"I've spent most of my life feeling like I can't get anything right. I'm the kind of person who keeps messing up again and again." She sighed. "I got myself into this mess, and I want to get myself out."

"But it isn't all your fault. What about the part Mark played in all of this?"

"He didn't make the decision to start a whole new life on a credit card."

"No, but he put you into the position to have to make that decision."

She chewed on her bottom lip and stared at him like she was thinking about something. "I guess you're right. I still want to find a way out of this myself though."

Adam dropped her off at her apartment. He sat in his car and watched her walk into her building. Anyone watching would've mistaken the bounce in her step for a sign of joy, but Adam knew she was walking in time to the beat that had been tormenting her for too long now. He hoped one of them would be able to figure out how to stop the music in her head before it drove her insane.

Chapter 2

Even though the music was driving her insane, the disco beat infected every move she made. Cheryl couldn't help but bounce a bit as she walked up the stairs to her apartment. She was due to start a shift on the psychic hotline soon but hoped to get some rest first. If only this music would leave her alone. She was disappointed to see him standing on the landing. He wore black bell bottom jeans and a black shirt with the type of sheen only unnatural fabrics have. His mahogany skin glistened with sweat, and his Afro was a bit uneven on one side. He stared down at her with a forlorn expression. Cheryl shook her head at him as she approached.

"What do you want from me?" she said aloud, not caring if the neighbors could hear her standing in the hall talking to herself. "You're ruining me with your music. I can't even think straight." She pointed her finger at him.

He looked at her, perplexed, but didn't say a word.

Cheryl stopped on the top step so there were only inches between them. "Why won't you talk to me? It would be so much easier if you did. Just tell me what you want, and I'll help you." Her voice quivered. Tears of frustration pricked her eyes. "I can't keep this up. You're driving me insane." She let out a small sarcastic laugh. "Okay, maybe I already am insane, but you're only making it worse."

He didn't react to anything she said.

"Stop looking at me like you don't approve." She jabbed her index finger at him, and he vanished. Unfortunately, the music didn't.

Her neighbor, Mr. Duncan, stuck his head outside his apartment door and scowled. "I don't care how early it is. You still shouldn't play your music that loud."

Cheryl opened her mouth to tell him that she wasn't playing any music, but before she could say anything he slammed his door shut again. She walked up to her apartment door and fumbled in her purse for her keys. Once she unlocked it, she pushed the door open and was not greeted like usual by her feline companion, Beau. Her apartment door led into a disco. She was familiar with the scene by now. She had watched it play out again and again, hopefully this time her disco ghost listened to her and would show her something she could do to help him.

Dancers filled the floor in bell bottom pants and polyester shirts. They sweated as they swung their hips and bounced to the beat. Cheryl looked over the crowd and saw her ghost bopping his head as he walked across the dance floor. He stopped to talk to a woman with long dark hair and tight gold pants. She laughed, showing her perfect, white teeth as she threw her head back. They danced together for a moment. He put his hands on her hips and swayed back and forth.

Cheryl caught sight of a short, pale man with dark brown hair and a mustache like a broom, watching them from the other side of the dance floor with a look of disgust on his face. Then he stormed out the front door. She wondered who he was. Should she follow him? No, she was there to see her ghost, the ghost in black.

When the song ended, the ghost in black whispered something in his dance partner's ear before continuing his journey across the dance floor. He weaved between the dancers to the other side of the room, disappearing down a hallway. Cheryl hurried after him. When she reached the hallway three doors confronted her. She had no idea which one he'd gone through. Then she heard the sound of metal scraping against metal, and she turned to see a column of smoke snaking around the dance floor. People screamed and ran. Others fell to the floor when the smoke coiled around them, taking the life from them. Chaos ensued. So many people ran and screamed that Cheryl couldn't keep track of who was around her. She needed to get to her ghost, the man in black, but the scene seemed so real that it was difficult to push through the crowd of people. Then she spotted him. The ghost she'd been following moved through the crowd in the opposite direction of everyone else. He swam against the crush of the people back to the center of the dance floor. Cheryl looked around, wondering where he was going. The throng of people pushed him back, yelling and crying, but he moved them aside and kept coming forward into the room, toward the smoke, toward death, toward Cheryl. Caught up in the fear and confusion of it all, she began to call out. "No! No!" Then the whole scene dropped away, and she was left standing just inside her apartment at the door with Beau sitting at her feet.

**

Adam pulled out of the parking space and started home. He worried about Cheryl. This new ghost was torturing her with music, and he didn't know how to help her stop it. He wondered if the shopkeeper could give him advice about what to do. As if summoned by the thought, the shop appeared on the corner. Adam recognized the telltale green door with the Enchantment sign hanging above it. "What the...?" he said to himself, craning his neck as he drove by.

He had to park his car a block away. When he got out, he practically ran to the bookstore. Part of him was afraid it would disappear again before he got there. Maybe it was a mirage, and he hadn't seen it at all. When he got to the storefront, the sign still hung over the door, green with gold letters. Would it be completely abandoned again and torn to pieces like it had been the last time he tried to go? He took a deep breath and pushed the door open. A chime sounded.

The store smelled of sandalwood. Crowded bookshelves lined the walls. In the center of the room, a table displayed trays of smooth gemstones.

Adam took a deep breath, relieved to see the store back in its original condition. He could still picture it in ruins like he had seen it only a month ago. The door behind the counter opened, and the shopkeeper strolled out on long legs.

"You're here." Adam couldn't hide his delight.

"So are you." A sly smile slid across the shopkeeper's slender face. His deep-set eyes danced with joy.

"I tried to come back before, but your shop had been abandoned."

The shopkeeper continued to smile at him. He blinked his dark eyes slowly. "Are you sure you were in the right place?"

The question made him doubt himself. "Yeah. I think so."

"I think so isn't sure." The shopkeeper smiled again, and every time he did, Adam felt less and less sure of himself. "You've been doing good work." He walked out from around the counter and slipped a book from the bookcase to his left without even looking. The other books on the shelf slumped over, taking up the vacant space the missing book left. "Have you been learning a lot? Did you finish the book I gave you?"

"How do you know what I've been doing?" Adam ignored his other questions.

"Some things are known." He flipped through the book in his hand absentmindedly. "Many of life's mysteries aren't mysteries at all. They are secrets that only the right people are permitted to know."

Adam scoffed. "And you're the right people?"

He nodded. "And so are you."

Adam shifted on his feet uncomfortably. He didn't feel like he was the kind of person who should be trusted with any of the world's mysteries.

The shopkeeper raised an eyebrow. "I sense some disagreement."

Adam shook his head. "I came here because I need some advice." He'd originally wanted to know if he could control his visions; Cheryl's situation was at the forefront of his mind. "My partner—"

"Oh yes. Cheryl."

Adam cocked his head at him. "I don't remember ever telling you her name."

"When will you realize that you don't have to tell me anything." He set the book on the counter and put his hands in his pockets. "Cheryl's having a mighty difficult time with that ghost, isn't she?"

"Yes, she is." He didn't want to think too much about how he knew this. "She can't seem to get him to tell her what he wants, and in the meantime he keeps pumping disco music into her head so she has a hard time doing anything else."

The shopkeeper clucked his tongue. "Sometimes those ghosts are so confused, they don't know how to get the help they need. He's stuck in a loop reliving the same moment in time again and again."

Adam waited, hoping he'd give him some insight. "How can she figure out what he needs to stop all of this?"

He shrugged. "That's not my specialty."

"What is your specialty?" Frustration rippled through him.

"Books, visions, counsel." His gaze fell on the book on the counter. He picked it up and held it out to Adam.

Adam looked down at another small paperback. He didn't know if he wanted to take it. Maybe he didn't want to know any more secrets. Learning what he had about himself in this short time had already been a lot. Reluctantly, he took the book. This one had an image of a horse running through a field on the front cover. The faded colors gave it a dreamlike quality. In white cursive scrawl, the title read The Secrets of Sight for the Gifted. He didn't even bother to flip through it.

"It is a good book. It will give you insights the other one is missing." He pressed his lips together like he was trying desperately not to say more.

"What's it about?" Adam asked.

"What's it about?" He chuckled when he repeated the question. "You'll find out when you read it." He smiled slyly. "When you need it, it will be there."

Adam looked down at the book again. "I guess I'll have to read it, then," he mumbled. He didn't appreciate how the shopkeeper never answered his questions directly, but he was glad to see he really did exist. If it wasn't for the first book he had given him, Adam might have been thoroughly convinced he'd only imagined the shopkeeper before.

"Yes, you will." He turned around and went back behind the counter. He squatted down out of Adam's sight.

Adam stood waiting for a while, thinking that he was getting something else to show him. After a few uncomfortable minutes, he walked over to the counter. He leaned across it to see the shopkeeper organizing shelves there. He looked up at Adam as if surprised that he was still there. "Is there something else you wanted?" he asked.

Adam shook his head. "I guess not."

"Until next time." The shopkeeper went back to shifting around the objects on the shelves.

"Until next time." Adam wasn't quite sure what he expected, but he left the shop feeling disappointed and confused. Each time he saw the shopkeeper, he seemed to end up with more questions than answers and another book. That shouldn't have been surprising because it was a bookstore after all. As he walked back up the street to his car, he wondered if this book would contain the answers he wanted about being a visionary and how to control what he saw.

Maybe he'd expected too much from the shopkeeper. He'd been so happy to see the shop and thought he'd go inside, and the shopkeeper would give him a magic key to unlock a way to make everything better for Cheryl. He was kidding himself. There were no magic keys.

He got into his car and was ready to start it when he looked up and saw the green door with the sign above it that said Enchantment on the storefront next to his car. It was all wrong. He had parked a block away from the store. He turned off his car and got out. This wasn't right. He ran his hand through his hair and looked to his left and to his right. People hurried by him like it was a normal day. He walked with the determined stride to the door and yanked it open.

The chime above the door sounded again. Calming New Age music floated through the air. The shopkeeper stood up from his squatting position behind the counter. "You're back?"

Adam looked around the shop with his hands on his hips. "What are you doing here?"

The shopkeeper raised an eyebrow at him. "This is my shop. What are you doing here?"

"I mean, what are you doing here?" Adam pointed at the ground. "I just came out of the store."

"That you did," the shopkeeper said.

Adam glared at him. "I just came out of the store a block up that way." He pointed to his right. "How are you here now?"

"Why do you expect the store to follow the same rules of time and space that you do? You're a smart man. You can see things that no one else can. Why do you hold on to the idea that this shop is in one particular place? The shop is everywhere at once." He held out his arms with a flourish.

Adam drew his eyebrows together. Thinking about this was making his head hurt. "Okay. But when you're dealing with me, can you just keep the shop in one place. It stresses me out, and I have a lot of stuff going on right now."

The shopkeeper leaned over the counter. "Like what?"

Adam shook his head before turning and walking to the door.

As he pulled it open, the shopkeeper said, "Don't forget to read that book."

Adam waved his hand over his head dismissively as he walked out of the store.

Chapter 3

Janet padded around her bedroom in her nightgown, preparing to go to sleep. She'd nearly finished the book on her nightstand and was looking forward to snuggling into bed and reading the last pages. She was picking out her clothes for the next day, something she'd always done, when she heard a noise in the hall. A gurgling bubbled through the air. Janet had become accustomed to ignoring noises in her house, but this one was worrisome. The house was old, and the plumbing wasn't always the best. She opened the bedroom door and listened. The sound grew louder. She flipped on the light and walked into the hall.

She swallowed hard when she realized the sound was coming from the bathroom she no longer used. Her armpits began to sweat. Her breath grew shallow. She stood, looking at the door with anxiety building in her chest. When she had finally convinced herself she needed to turn around and go back to the bedroom, she noticed something slipping beneath the bathroom door. A black viscous fluid oozed onto the hardwood floor. The sharp scent of sulfur found its way to her nostrils.

She gasped. Was sewage backing up into her bathroom?

She couldn't ignore it. She had to do something. Hesitantly, she stepped forward, approaching the door. The goo rolled toward her. Then it seemed to come together forming a shape—a hand. It reached for her ankle, and Janet jumped back, narrowly escaping its grasp. She hurried to the top of the stairs, shrieking.

As soon as the sound left her mouth, she heard someone call her name. "Mrs. Tate, are you okay?" The night nurse rushed from Frank's room to the bottom of the stairs. "What happened?"

Janet looked back at the bathroom door, and the black goo was gone. It had disappeared. Maybe it had been a figment of her imagination. "Nothing. I just saw a palmetto bug."

The nurse crinkled her face with disapproval. "I thought you were dying." She shook her head. "You about scared the life out of me. Though I hate those too."

"They're just terrible, aren't they?" Janet glanced over her shoulder again. The floor was clean. "Sorry about that."

"No problem. Good night." The nurse turned, disappearing into Frank's room again.

Janet walked back over to the bathroom door and looked down at the floor. There was no evidence anything had been there. She squatted and ran her hand along the smooth blond wood floor. "You're not going to drive me crazy. I'm going to figure out what you are and get rid of you," she whispered at the door.

She stood and went to her bedroom to read, not knowing that the force had entered her home wouldn't be defeated as easily as she hoped.

***

Cheryl sat on the floor with her legs crossed and her back

resting against the couch. The cards on the coffee table in front of her only had good messages for the client on the other end of the line. Unfortunately, her client seemed to only want bad news.

"Are you sure? What you're saying doesn't sound right to me because I found the receipt in his pocket for a bouquet of roses. He didn't give me any roses." The woman's voice was sharp. She had called to see if her longtime boyfriend had been cheating on her. The cards said no, but she wasn't convinced that easily.

"I can only tell you what the cards say. The cards are telling me this is all a misunderstanding. All you need to do is talk to him about it. That means stop sneaking around and searching his phone and looking in his pockets and ask him what's going on." This advice seemed obvious to Cheryl.

The woman sucked her teeth. "You act like he'll tell me the truth. Nobody's going to tell the truth about something like that."

"It sounds to me like you want to catch him cheating. I'm not sure why that would be, but if you're looking for an excuse to break off the relationship, you don't need one. If things aren't working out for you, break up with him."

The woman sighed heavily. "Every guy I've ever dated has cheated on me. I'm afraid this one is too. I don't want to get hurt again." For the first time during the call the woman's voice softened, and Cheryl knew she was being completely honest.

"When you've been hurt over and over again like you have, it's hard to trust someone with your heart. Believe me, I understand, but if you stay closed off and always expect the worst, you'll never experience the joy of falling in love completely again. It's scary to trust people, and you could get hurt, but those are the risks we have to take if we want to experience the fullness of life." Cheryl felt like she was giving herself advice.

"So the cards are saying I need to trust him." The woman spoke softly.

"You need to talk to him. Ask him what's going on."

"But what if he is cheating?" Her voice broke.

"The cards say he's not. But if the cards are wrong and he is, it's better that you know for sure, so you can move on with life. Right now, you're stuck in a worried and anxious state. Life is too short to stay stuck like that for too long. The best thing to do is find out for sure, but the cards are telling me you're going to be surprised by the answer because what's going on is not what you think."

Usually, Cheryl's clients didn't need that much convincing, but once the call was over, she was glad she had the chance to ease the woman's mind. She wasn't quite sure if the woman would follow her advice, but she thought the advice she gave her was good. She put away her tarot cards and packed up her headset before moving on to the sofa. When she looked at her cell phone, she saw she had thirteen missed calls. They were all from unknown numbers. She had decided to ignore all her credit card bills and just concentrate on being able to pay her utilities and her rent ages ago. That meant credit card companies were calling her constantly. At first, the whole situation made her so worried she was often sick to her stomach, but now she had numbed herself to it.

The disco music in her head was quiet for now. She sat back and closed her eyes. In the past, she had never truly appreciated silence like she did now. That silence didn't last long. Someone started knocking at her door.

Whack. Whack. Whack.

It was early, and she was still in her pajamas even though she had been working. She looked down at her oversized T-shirt and faded shorts, and decided she wasn't going to answer the door. Then the person knocked again.

Whack. Whack. Whack.

"I know you're in there." It was Mr. Duncan.

She sighed and got up. She ambled over to the door, hoping he'd be gone by the time she opened it. He wasn't. He stood with his dog Daisy at his side. He wore a pair of brick-colored Bermuda shorts and yellow paisley short-sleeve shirt. "When I started hearing your music at two in the morning, I thought she must want me to call the police and file a noise complaint against her. Is that what you want?"

She understood Mr. Duncan's frustration. She was feeling it too. "Of course I don't want you to call the police, but I promise you the music isn't coming from me."

He narrowed his eyes at her. "It certainly sounds like it is."

"I know. I'm sorry it's keeping you up, but it's not me. If you feel like you need to call the police, I guess you should go ahead and do that." Her phone began to buzz on the coffee table, and she turned and looked at it.

Maybe it was the fact that she seemed so resigned, but Mr. Duncan decided to tone down his anger. "Don't let it happen again," he said.

Cheryl nodded. She wished she could make a promise like that, but she had no control over it. "Okay. Enjoy your morning walk." She closed the door before he could say anything else. The last thing she wanted to do was fight with any of her neighbors. This ghost was ruining so many things in her life. She hoped it would all get better soon, but usually, things got worse before they ever got better.

Chapter 4

Adam rang the doorbell of the white two-story home. They stood on the concrete porch and waited for Janet Tate to answer. "What did she tell you when she called?" Cheryl asked.

Janet had called Adam earlier that morning, her voice tinged with panic. Adam shrugged. "Not much of anything. She said something strange happened in the bathroom, and she was a bit freaked out. She didn't go into details though. I told her we'd come and check the cameras to see what they recorded." He rapped on the door again.

"Did you notice anything when you were in the bathroom?" Cheryl asked.

Adam shook his head. "Not really. I guess it smelled funny."

Just then, Janet opened the door. "Thank you for coming." She stepped to the side so they could enter.

It was unseasonably hot, and Adam was grateful to get inside out of the sun. The house was cool, and Janet had left the gauzy curtains over the windows in the living room closed. Just a bit of light filtered in. "You said something came out of the bathroom and attacked you." Adam paused and looked at her, waiting for Janet to tell him the story in more detail. She looked around as if keeping a secret from someone. Then she stepped close to them and, in a loud whisper, said, "When I was going to bed last night, I heard a noise. So I went into the hallway to investigate, and there was something coming out from under the bathroom door. It was some kind of sludge or something. It was pretty disgusting. Then it turned into a hand and reached for me." She grabbed hold of Adam's forearm as if demonstrating what a hand grabbing you might feel like. Her plump fingers dug into his flesh. Then she let go just as quickly as she had grabbed him. Her face flushed. "I'm sorry. I got carried away. That happens sometimes. Frank always says..." Her voice trailed off.

"What does Frank always say?" Cheryl asked.

"Nothing." She turned her head again, looking behind her toward the hall that led to Frank's room. "He was always such a good storyteller, much better than me."

"You're doing a great job so far. We need as many details as possible—the more, the better." Adam looked at the dim hallway. "How is your husband today?"

Janet shook her head. "He's not so good today. He didn't even know who I was this morning. Sometimes I wonder if it's the medication messing with his mind or the illness."

"It might be a combination of the two," Adam said. "I'm going to check the cameras and see if there's anything on them. Is that okay?"

Janet nodded.

Adam walked past her toward the back hallway. "I'll start with the one upstairs."

Cheryl followed him, leaving Janet standing in the living room with her arms crossed. As they approached Frank's room, a chill ran down Adam's spine. There was something strange in the house this time. He couldn't quite put his finger on what it was, but it felt like the energy in the entire house had been rearranged. "Do you feel that?" he whispered to Cheryl.

She shook her head. "I have a hard time sensing much of anything anymore."

"The dance party in your head is still going on?"

"Why wouldn't it be?" She scowled.

It took Janet a moment, but eventually, she followed them up the stairs to check the hallway camera. When they watched the tiny screen, it showed exactly what Janet had described. She came out of her room into the hallway and saw something on the floor. Startled, she jumped back. The picture was too small to see if there was anything on the floor though. Adam couldn't make anything out. He took the memory card out of the camera and slipped a new one in. "I'll have to take a look at this on a bigger screen to see what's on the floor."

"When you do, you'll definitely see it," Janet said.

Adam went to the bathroom door and opened it. When he did, Janet jumped back like she expected something to rush out at her, but nothing did. "Let's see if we got anything on this one." He took the camera facing the mirror over the vanity off its tripod.

Cheryl stepped into the bathroom with him, and Janet stayed in the hall standing against the wall opposite the door. "There's no way I'm going in there."

"We can watch it out there." Adam walked out into the hallway.

Janet shook her head. "I don't think I want to see what's on it." She covered her mouth with her hand. "I don't feel so good."

Cheryl walked over and put her hand on Janet's shoulder. "You don't have to watch anything you don't want to."

Adam stood opposite her near the bathroom door. He started playing the video before Cheryl came back over to watch it with him. Though the camera had turned on as if there was movement somewhere, the image it caught showed nothing interesting at first. It was only a camera recording a reflection of itself. Then a few dots of light crossed in front of the lens, and a single hand reached out of the glass of the mirror. Its charred skin cracked as the joints moved, revealing the tender pink flesh beneath it. It eased itself out of the mirror. A tenuous forearm followed by an upper arm and a shoulder came into view. Adam's mouth dropped open, and Cheryl gipped his arm. Just when he thought whoever it was would reveal its face to the camera, the video went black. Adam and Cheryl looked at each other, unsure about what they just saw. They ran it back and watched it again, one time, two times, three times.

Eventually, Janet was curious. "I don't like the look on your faces. What is it?"

He shook his head. "I'm not sure."

"It looks like something crawled out of your bathroom mirror." Cheryl stated it like this was something that happened every day.

"I told you. I told you I saw someone in that mirror that wasn't me." Tears flowed from Janet's eyes. "I'm not crazy."

"Do you want to see the video?" Cheryl asked her.

She shook her head. "I've already seen him more times than I want to. I don't need to see him again. In fact, life would be better if I never saw him again. That's why I hired you."

Adam understood the sentiment. Every time a ghost appeared, you'd hope it was the last time. Unfortunately, it usually wasn't.

He replaced the memory card in this camera too. "I'll leave this set up and see what else we get."

"What are you going to do to get rid of it?" Janet asked.

"First, we have to figure out what it is. Then we can get rid of it," Cheryl said.

"So, you expect me to sleep here when I know a ghost has crawled out of my mirror and is roaming around my house?" She motioned toward the bathroom door with her hand.

Cheryl took a few steps closer to her. "I know this is all very upsetting, but you've been sleeping here this long, and you've been okay. These things build over time, and you seem to be in the early stages of a haunting. It will be scary, but you'll probably be okay."

Janet frowned. "Probably?"

A scream cut through the air.

Adam rushed out of the bathroom into the hallway to join Cheryl and Janet. "What was that?" Cheryl and Janet asked in unison.

The scream happened again, and they all hurried up the hallway and down the stairs. It was coming from Frank's room. When they stepped inside, they saw Frank thrashing about on his bed. He had thrown his bedding to the floor and was beating his hands against the bed's railings as he yelled.

"What's happening?" Janet directed her question at the nurse, who was filling the syringe from a vial of clear liquid.

"He's just feeling a bit agitated." The nurse spoke in a calm, measured tone. "I'm going to give him some of this to calm him down, so he doesn't hurt himself." After filling the syringe, she turned her attention back to Frank. Even though he was yelling, she continued to talk in a soft voice. "You're okay. You need to stop this and relax. Everything is going to be all right if you relax. Look," she pointed at Janet. "Your wife is here."

Janet took that as a cue for her to talk. "You have to calm down, Frank, or you'll hurt yourself, like Yvette says. Just relax. It's going to be okay. I know this is hard. I know you're hurting, but you have to calm down." Her voice cracked. She couldn't keep the same measured calm that Yvette displayed. As she spoke her face seemed to crumble until she was speaking through sobs.

Adam looked up over the bed and saw the ceiling split. A black hole yawned open over the hospital bed. What looked like hundreds of white skeletal arms reached out of the darkness. He couldn't tell if they were trying to escape or trying to grab hold of Frank and pull him up. He watched the scene in shocked horror. Pointing at the commotion, he said to Cheryl, "Can you see that?"

"The ghost I saw the other day is here." Her eyes opened wide. With a determined stride, she marched around the hospital bed to the other side.

"Come over here and give me a hand," Yvette motioned for Adam to join her at Frank's bedside.

It took a moment for Adam to realize she was talking to him because he was so focused on what was going on above the hospital bed. He hurried over to the bedside, and the nurse directed him and Cheryl on how to help her restrain Frank so she could give him his injection. As soon as she pulled the needle from Frank's arm, the hole in the ceiling closed up, sucking the arms back into it before disappearing completely. Cheryl and Adam looked at each other across the hospital bed. "Well, that was something," Adam said to her, his voice deadpan.

"It certainly was," Cheryl answered.

Chapter 5

Cheryl was still rattled from what she'd seen at the Tate house as she rode back in the car with Adam. Her mind was all over the place, and the music that was still playing in her head didn't help much. "I can't imagine how terrible this whole situation must be for her." Cheryl stared out the window as they turned onto a busy street. "They must've been married for a long time, and now to watch him slowly decline like that… It's heartbreaking. I feel desperately sad every time we walk into that house."

Adam glanced over at her. "My parents were just gone one day without warning. At least, they have time together before he dies."

"Yeah, but at least you didn't have to see your parents suffer."

"That's true, but I didn't get to say goodbye either." The muscles in his jaw tensed.

"Losing someone is losing someone. No matter how it happens, it's devastating." She chewed on her bottom lip. "It must've been so hard for you and Jules. She went from being a normal college student to having to raise her younger brother. Not that you're a burden or anything. I'm not trying to say that."

"I know what you mean." Adam thought for a moment. "It was hard for both of us in different ways."

"I didn't really know my father. So, when he died, I didn't feel like I was losing much of anything." She paused. "No, that's not true. I felt like I was losing the chance to make amends with him. The fantasy of the relationship we could've had vanished once he was gone. And when my mom died... Well, we didn't have much of a relationship by then. She wasn't very happy with me. She had never been, but once I was with Mark, it got particularly bad. I understand that now, but I thought the way she disapproved of him was just another way for her to try to control me. I guess I was wrong about that."

"You can't be right about everything."

"Yeah, but when it came to Mark, I wasn't right about anything."

He drove along in silence for a few moments, listening to the rumble of the tires on the road. Each of them was lost in their thoughts.

"What do you think that was on the video?" Adam asked.

Cheryl hadn't thought about it since she'd seen it because her mind was so full of other things. "It wasn't the ghost I keep seeing in Frank's room. It was something else."

"Something?" He emphasized the word.

"It doesn't seem like an ordinary ghost to me. I can't say for sure, but it's a feeling I have. It's something else." She slowed down her speech to emphasize each word. When she closed her eyes, she could see the charred hand reaching toward her. She opened her eyes and shook her head as if trying to shake the image from her mind.

"What did you see in Frank's room? Because I saw the

ceiling open up and a bunch of bony arms reaching down. It was like they were trying to grab Frank and pull him up through the hole."

"I didn't see that at all. I saw the ghost again. It was the same one I saw before." In her mind, she saw him again so clearly. His long narrow face looked so forlorn. "He has a message for us."

"Why hasn't he told it to us yet?"

Cheryl thought for a moment. "We've only been there twice. Maybe he doesn't trust us yet. Maybe he doesn't realize I can see him."

"Next time we go, you have to talk to him."

"I know. There's just so much going on in my head that it's hard to concentrate. Next time, I definitely will." She needed to solve the disco ghost's problem so she could be more clearheaded.

The phone rang. Adam looked at her. "It's Jules," he said to her before answering it. "Hey, sis, how are you doing?"

"You sound like you're in a good mood." Her voice blasted through the speakers.

"How can I not be when I'm talking to you. Cheryl's with me."

"Cheryl, how are you?"

"Good." Cheryl had only talked to Jules on the phone once before.

"I'm glad you're both here. I want to invite you for dinner tomorrow night. You too, Cheryl." The high-pitched laughter of children chimed in the background.

"I'm sorry, Jules, but I have to work, so I won't be able to make it." Cheryl fiddled absentmindedly with the silver bangles on her wrist. Adam had tried to get her to meet Jules before. She knew she would have to meet her eventually, but she just wasn't up to it right now.

"Maybe we could do it another night, then. Just tell me what would work for you." Jules's voice continued to sound cheery.

Cheryl shot Adam a panicked look before answering. "Oh, I don't know. I've been working so much. Between my regular tarot readings and the psychic hotline and everything going on with Suncoast Paranormal..."

"And she hasn't been feeling very good recently either," Adam cut in. She was relieved to see that he was helping her come up with an excuse not to have dinner.

"Oh no." Jules had genuine concern in her voice. "What's wrong?"

Cheryl had no idea how she should answer this question, but Adam jumped in again.

"She's been getting a lot of headaches and can't focus." He winked at her.

"I'm so sorry to hear that. Have you seen a doctor?"

Cheryl wanted to laugh. She couldn't picture herself walking into a doctor's office and telling them she heard constant dance music in her head and couldn't get anything done. It was not like she could afford to see a doctor anyway. It had been ages since she'd had health insurance. "No," she said. "I think if I get enough rest, it should go away."

"Make sure you take care of yourself, then. Your health is your most valuable asset," Jules said.

Cheryl knew her health was her only asset.

"I can come over for dinner," Adam added after a lapse in the conversation.

"Good. Well, at least I'll get to see you tomorrow night. I was hoping to finally get to meet Cheryl though."

"We'll have to get together when things slow down for me." Cheryl could hear the excited voices of children in the background.

"Definitely." She paused. "Adam, Chloe's been begging me to tell you to come over. She misses her uncle. Isn't that right, Chloe?"

A small voice cheered in the background.

"I miss her too."

"We'll see you—Carson, no!" Jules spoke sternly.

Then someone began to cry. "Mom!" the children wailed together.

"I have to go before they tear down the whole house," Jules said breathlessly. "Sorry." She hung up.

Adam raised an eyebrow at Cheryl.

"They sound like a handful," she said.

"They are, but they're great."

She saw how his eyes shone when he talked about his niece and nephew. "You'd make a good dad."

He glanced over at her before returning his eyes to the road. "Thanks. You'd make a good mom."

She shook her head. "I don't think so. I'm too flighty." That was how her mother had always described her, and she must've been right. She was so flighty that she'd made a complete disaster of her finances and was barely holding on to her sanity.

"You're not flighty. You're a free thinker."

Cheryl laughed. "That's one way of putting it."

"Seriously though, you're not flighty at all. You're almost always on time. You're responsible. And I think you would make a great mother."

"Thanks, but enough with the mother stuff. You're making me feel weird."

"Just one more thing." He held up his index finger. "Do you want kids?" He looked over at her again.

The question shocked her. Wasn't it too early in their relationship for all of this talk about children and what kind of parents they'd be? There was a time when she would've said yes to wanting to be a mother, but now she wasn't sure. "I don't know." She rolled the idea around in her mind as if she'd never thought of it before. "I don't think I want to be responsible for messing someone up."

"Who says you'd mess them up?"

She shrugged. "Mark taught me that the world is a dangerous place."

"What are you saying?" He turned down her street.

"I don't want to be responsible for anyone hurting." She chewed on the soft flesh on the inside of her cheek.

"That's not possible. Considering all the people you come into contact with, you're bound to hurt someone. It might not be intentional, but for the other person, it would still be painful."

"I realize that, but I want to avoid as much harm as possible." She continued chewing on the inside of her cheek.

"What's that have to do with having kids?"

She thought for a moment. "Bringing kids into the world would be bringing into being more people I could hurt."

"You've gone through a lot in your life, but you still have a life. Would you wish it away?"

She shook her head. "Sometimes—"

He looked over at her with shock on his face. "Cheryl?"

"Let me finish." She took a deep breath. "Sometimes, I wonder what I would be like if I hadn't experienced everything I have. I'd be a completely different version of myself. I like who I am now, even though I'm a mess. I've learned a lot of important lessons over the years." She tried to imagine herself as a different woman who'd lived a life free of hardships. She couldn't even picture what that might look like. "Would you change your past?"

He thought for a moment. "I've wondered how my life

would've been different if my parents were still alive, but not so much anymore. I'm not interested in hanging onto the past. My life has turned out pretty good. I have a good job. I have a beautiful girlfriend." He smiled slyly at her, and she grew flush. "I am doing something I love. The only thing that would make my life any better would be having a family of my own."

Cheryl nodded. Even though she wasn't ready for a family yet and her life was far from perfect, she knew what he meant. Her phone rang in her purse, but she didn't even bother to look at it. She already knew what the call was. "My life would be better if I had a million dollars."

He laughed. "Money won't magically solve all your problems." He pulled up in front of her building.

"It might not solve yours, but it would definitely solve a few of mine." The disco beat in her head had been muffled, but as soon as they stopped in front of her building, the volume seemed to crank up to eleven. She winced.

"Are you okay?" he asked.

She nodded. "I'm probably going to walk into a dance party when I open the door to my place. I don't really have time for this."

"Good luck," he said as she got out of the car. During the next few days, Cheryl would need all the help she could find.

***

Cheryl's phone rang as she walked up the stairs to her apartment. She pulled her keys from her purse, ignoring the vibrating phone. As soon as she stepped inside, her tabby cat, Beau, ran up to her. He placed his paws on her shins, looked up at her with his yellow-green eyes, and meowed.

"I missed you too." She scooped him up. His soft body

draped over her hand. She cradled him in her arms, and he began to purr. "You're such a sweet boy."

The music still throbbed in her brain. It was quieter than it had been, but it was still there, a constant reminder of a problem that needed solving. She sat on the sofa with Beau in her arms. The unopened pink envelope on the end table caught her attention for a moment, sending her thoughts racing. She couldn't think about this now. She needed to get this ghost out of her head. Until she did that, she'd have a hard time making any money at all.

She closed her eyes, petted Beau's head, and tried to relax.

She felt the ghost watching her. He was standing right in front of her now. She knew it without even looking. The hair on her arms stood on end, and a chill ran down her back. She opened her eyes slowly and wasn't surprised by what she saw. He stood in front of her in a black shirt and black bell-bottom jeans. His Afro was like a cloud on top of his head. He stared at her with large gentle eyes.

"What do you need from me?" She waited for an answer.

He stood in front of her staring into her soul.

Cheryl's eyes drifted down to the pocket of his jeans. She could already see the dark wet stain spreading. He reached his hand inside, and she knew what would happen. She heard the squelch of him grabbing at raw flesh. Then he pulled the red lump from his pocket. He held a still-beating human heart out to her. Veins covered its glistening surface. Cheryl flinched, expecting him to throw it at her like he did last time. He didn't. He only held it in the palm of his outstretched hand as he looked deep into her eyes.

"I don't understand. What are you trying to tell me?" she asked.

Then the music came back. It swelled in her thoughts. Her apartment dropped away and turned into a dance club. The crowd of people danced around her. Her sofa sat right in the middle of the dance floor. The man threw the heart straight up in the air. Cheryl followed its flight with her eyes and then somehow lost sight of it. It seemed to have vanished. When she lowered her gaze back to the man, he was walking away, blood from the heart still dripping from his fingertips. He left a red speckled trail on the floor as he went.

Cheryl set Beau on the couch next to her and got up to follow the man. She followed the drips of blood on the floor. Some of it was smeared beneath the dancers' shoes. The man in black stopped at a couple and seemed to ask them a question. Together they all craned their neck looking around the dance floor before the man in black walked away from them. He searched the crowd as if looking for someone, leaving a trail of blood dripping from his fingertips behind as he went. She followed it into a dimly lit hallway, past the bathrooms, and to the door at the back of the club. The red handprint on the scuffed navy blue door marked his trail. Cheryl swallowed a lump in her throat, took a deep breath, and pushed the door open.

Cheryl peered out into a dark alley. Lightning flashed in the distance, lighting up the sky. The man in black was nowhere to be seen. Cheryl stepped outside. The heavy metal door slammed shut and the music inside muffled. "Hello? Where are you?" she called out to the man in black. She strained her eyes in the darkness. She was alone in the alley. Thinking her ghost was probably back inside she turned to open the door only to find it locked.

"Darn it." She yanked at it again, hoping she could use brute strength to open it, but she could not. "None of this is real. None of this is real." She repeated the words, trying to keep herself calm. Standing there in the dark she took a few deep breaths. She knew at any moment all of this would drop away and she would be back in her apartment. She walked up the alley in the dark, feeling the lumpy bricks through the thin soles of her sandals. Lightning flashed, momentarily lighting her way. When she got to the end of the alley, she looked up the street and saw the silhouette of a church spire in front of her.

"Wait a minute." She spun around, paying attention to what little she could see around her in the darkness. Then the scene dropped away, and Cheryl was in her apartment again. Beau lay curled up on the sofa where she had left him. Her room was bathed in warm light.

Cheryl grabbed her keys and ran out her front door. She rushed down the stairs and burst out of the apartment building like she was late for something. She ran to the corner and then turned left and ran to the spot where the alley behind her building met the main road. A pickup truck driving too quickly up the narrow alley honked at her, and she jumped out of the way of its bright headlights.

"I can't believe it," she said to herself as she stood looking at the same brick church across the street that she had seen in the alley by the disco. She turned and looked at her apartment building. It was an old building. Part of the reason she was renting there was because she liked the character of the place. Was is it possible that this place was once the disco? She had too many questions and still not enough answers.

***

Janet sat on the sofa with her head in her hands. The television was on, but the volume was muted. Two women yelled at each other on the screen in a busy bar as a crowd gathered around them. The camera pushed in on their faces, inches from one another. Janet turned off the television. She ran her hands through her dark hair. She still hadn't managed to get to the hairdresser to get her roots done. She knew the video the camera recorded in the bathroom would terrify her, so she hadn't looked at it when she had the chance. Now she wished she had. She was probably making it all worse than it was. She kept imagining a murderous creature covered in slime crawling from the bathroom mirror. Was it still in the house? Would she see it crawling down the stairs, a twisted body on stilt-like legs, coming to devour her? She shuddered at the thought.

"Mrs. Tate, are you okay?" Yvette stood behind her with her oversized purse slung over her shoulder.

"Yeah, I'm fine. Just shaken up, that's all." Janet got up from the sofa.

"I know this is hard for you. It would be for anyone. As the illness progresses, his mind will continue to degrade, and it will only get more difficult. It might be better for you if we transfer him to a facility." Yvette had walked into the living room and was standing next to the coffee table.

Of course, Yvette would think she was shaken by Frank's outburst earlier, but it was so much more than that. "That's not what he wanted."

"I know, but you have to consider your sanity too. And you could end up getting hurt when you're here alone with him." She looked at Janet with kind brown eyes.

"It'll be okay. I can handle it." She crossed her arms and uncrossed them again. Secretly she knew she wasn't up to it, but she had promised Frank he wouldn't die in a hospital, and she intended to keep that promise.

Yvette pressed her lips together like she wanted to say more but thought better of it. She shifted her bag from one shoulder to the other. "Well, I'm off for the night. You should put in for more night shift nurses. You shouldn't be alone with him." She looked at Janet with concern.

Janet smiled weakly. "I'll be fine." She wasn't certain of that.

"I'll be back in the morning, first thing. "

"Good night, Yvette." Janet walked her to the door and locked it behind her.

It was getting dark. Janet hated this time in the old house alone with Frank and their ghosts. Was there only one? She turned the television back on, turning up the volume. The noise made her feel safer, even though she knew it didn't protect her from anything at all. The less she heard in the house, the better. She padded through the living room, then down the hallway to Frank's room. He lay in his bed with his head slightly inclined. He opened his eyes.

"You're awake." She spoke cautiously, not knowing what she would do if he became agitated again.

He moistened his chapped lips with his tongue. "It looks like I am."

Janet went into the room and picked up the glass of water from the bedside table, offering it to him. He sat up a bit more, and she held the straw to his lips so he could take a sip. "Today was a rough day."

He nodded in agreement as he swallowed the water down. "I don't remember much of it."

"That's probably for the best."

"I was that bad, huh?" His honey-colored eyes sparkled with mischief.

She couldn't help but smile. "Yeah, it was pretty intense." Janet held on to any inkling of the man he used to be. The few lucid moments she had with him were a treasure. She was so grateful for their conversations in these moments.

"It's only going to get worse," a disembodied voice seemed to whisper in her ear. "What?" she asked.

"I didn't say anything."

"You just told me it would get worse." The creases between her eyebrows deepened.

He shook his head. "I didn't say that, but we both know it's true. I'm dying. It's all downhill from here." He tried to smile, but the grin did not reach his eyes.

"I'm serious, Frank. I just heard someone say it's only going to get worse." Her heart hammered in her chest.

"Maybe you heard my thoughts. We've been married so long you can read my mind." He was still smiling at her.

"This isn't funny, Frank. Someone said something to me. If it wasn't you, who was it?" She walked over to the closet and yanked the door open, revealing the shelf with extra sheets and blankets. She bent down and looked underneath the hospital bed.

"What are you doing?" Frank was trying to sit up now but doing so wore him out.

"There's someone else in the house. He just spoke to me." She marched out of the room. "I'm going to find him."

"Janet, what are you doing?" Frank called after her as she marched into the hallway. She checked the back door to make sure it was locked. It was. Then she went through the downstairs, checking all the closets. Once she had checked every inch of the house except the bathroom, she went back to Frank's room to find him asleep. She stood next to his bed, her hands resting on the rails at the side of the bed. His eyelids opened slightly, revealing narrow slits of his eyes. "Did you find anyone?" His voice was hoarse.

"No, there's no one else in the house. Not that I can find anyway."

He reached up and put his hand on hers. His skin was dry and fragile as onion skin. "I love you, Janet Tate."

"I love you too, Frank Tate." She wiped the tears from her

face. She watched as he drifted off to sleep again. She feared each lucid moment would be the last. There were so few now that she treasured each one.

Too fearful to go upstairs, Janet slept on the sofa that night. She pulled the thin multicolored blanket that usually laid over the back of the couch up over her shoulders as she curled up in front of the television. She left the television on, the bright colors casting a glow into the room to keep her company. From the living room, she could hear Frank snoring.

Once she woke in the middle of the night with the distinct feeling someone had been standing over her, watching her. It was like she saw the person in a dream. A balding man, so tall his head nearly touched the ceiling. The bones in his cheek were prominent, giving his face his squarish look. He stared down at her, watching. He opened his mouth like he was going to tell her something. She had the feeling what he had to say was very important, but no sound came out. When she opened her eyes, she was convinced she would see him standing over her, but there was no one there.

The television was on like it had been before. Frank's snoring marked out a gentle rhythm of sleep from the next room. Janet closed her eyes and did her best to get back to sleep.

Chapter 6

Cheryl looked up from the cards on the table. "You already know what you need to do, Shonda. We talk about this every time you come here. Your reading has been almost the same for months." She didn't usually like to have this tone with her clients, but Shonda was a regular who needed some convincing to act.

"I know, but I'm waiting for the time to be right." She pushed her long black braids behind her shoulder. She was so young. Her full round face shone with an innocent enthusiasm Cheryl wished she still had.

"The time will never be perfect. The perfect time to start something is whenever you decide to start it. It's time to move forward with the book you said you wanted to write. Look at the cards." Cheryl's voice rose as she motioned to the cards. "They keep telling you this is the time to nurture your creative energy." She picked up the Magician card and showed it to Shonda. A man in a red cloak stood against a yellow background with a wand raised, an infinity symbol floating above his head. She put the card back on the table. "Right now, everything is aligned for you to have success in whatever you pursue, so why not pursue the thing you said you always wanted." Shonda had been talking about her book idea ever since the first day she came to see Cheryl.

She nodded as she put her purse on the table and pulled out her wallet. "I know. I know. I'm just afraid of not being good enough." She pulled out her phone and checked the time.

"We're all afraid of not being good enough. You won't know if you don't start. If you never write your book, how will you ever become a better writer?" Cheryl tried to make eye contact with her, but she nodded, pulled money from her wallet, and counted it without looking up.

She slid the cash across the table to Cheryl. "I know you're right about just getting started. I will. I'll start tonight."

Cheryl had heard this from her before. "Don't just say it. Do it this time."

She looked at Cheryl and gave a firm nod. "I will. I promise you. I don't break the promises I make to other people."

Cheryl took the money and counted it quickly. "It's more important not to break the promises you make yourself."

Shonda let a puff of air out of her nose. "Okay. I'll remember that one. I have to go. My lunch break is over."

"Hurry. I don't want you to be late because of me."

Once Shonda was gone, Cheryl got up and walked around the screen that divided the area where she gave readings from the rest of Day's shop. She was getting hungry. Stephanie walked in the door just as Shonda left.

"I was thinking Thai food from the place around the corner," Stephanie said, holding a finger in the air.

"Hello to you too." Cheryl walked over and gave her friend a hug.

"You know I only think about food when I'm hungry. All

civility goes out the window," Stephanie said.

Day wasn't in the store today. Instead, J.P., a stocky man with a jet black mohawk and a septum piercing, worked behind the counter. When Cheryl first met him, she was surprised Day had hired someone like him. She was so concerned with looking professional. After spending a little time with him, Cheryl understood why he got the job. He was sharp, smart, and reliable.

"I'm off to lunch," Cheryl said to him. "Do you want me to bring anything back for you?"

He stopped dusting the bookcase and thought for a moment. "Nah. I'm good."

"Okay. I'll be back soon." Cheryl followed Stephanie out the door. The Thai restaurant was only a few blocks away. It was an unbearably humid day, and even though the walk was short, Cheryl found herself sweating before they arrived at their destination. The air conditioning in the restaurant greeted her like an old friend.

Cheryl was glad when Stephanie decided to move back to St. Pete after her experience with the haunting in Sarasota. She liked having her best friend close by again so they could have lunches together. After they ordered their food, Stephanie leaned across the table and said in a loud whisper, "So, how's it going with your dancing ghost?"

"I've actually had a breakthrough. The other day, he showed me that the disco he keeps showing me was in my apartment building. I have to do some research. I've just been so busy, and it seems like whenever I have downtime, he's filling my head with disco so I can't think straight. Needless to say, I haven't gotten around to it yet." Cheryl was feeling so much pressure these days. As if on cue, her phone rang in her bag.

"Aren't you get that?" Stephanie asked.

"No, I'm not."

Stephanie nodded knowingly. They had discussed Cheryl's financial problems before, and she knew continuing to talk about them wouldn't make them go away. Cheryl didn't want to talk about them anyway. "If you need help with research, I can do that. I need a way to spend my spare time besides sitting at home thinking about Will. I still can't believe I was married to that monster."

Cheryl was just glad she was able to help Stephanie get out of the situation before it got bad. "If you could look up a few things for me, that would be helpful."

"Sure. Just tell me what you want to know."

Cheryl watched as an eight-year-old boy darted into the center of the restaurant with his hands outstretched to catch a ball. He passed right through the waitress who walked over to their table carrying plate loads of food. Stephanie followed her gaze, twisting in her chair to look at the center of the restaurant just as the waitress set their food on the table. They both ordered noodles, and steam rose from their plates. When the waitress left, Stephanie asked, "Is someone over there?"

"Yeah, there's a kid. He's eight, and he's playing ball. He's with that couple." She nodded in the direction of a couple in their late thirties on the other side of the restaurant eating silently. Cheryl wondered why the boy was still hanging around with the living. He didn't have the sorrowful demeanor that many of the ghosts she saw had. He seemed to be enjoying his time running around the restaurant.

Stephanie turned her attention back to Cheryl. "Are you going to go talk to him?"

Cheryl shook her head. "He doesn't seem to need anything. I think he's fine."

"I thought if they were still here, they weren't fine. If a ghost is fine, don't they just move on?"

The boy ran back over to the table where the couple sat.

"I can't just walk over to them and say, 'I can see a ghost around you, and this is what the ghost has to say.' Most people just aren't ready for that. To be honest, it's emotionally stressful for me too." She tried to imagine herself getting up from the table and approaching the couple and couldn't see a way of doing it that wouldn't make everyone upset. "I just don't want to ruin other people's day."

"But would you be ruining it? Maybe all they want to know is that whoever this child is to them is okay." Stephanie twisted around in her seat again to look at the couple. "They look so sad."

She was right. They did. "They do, but we all need boundaries. Sometimes I cross boundaries I have no business stepping over. I'm learning that."

Seemingly content with Cheryl's explanation, Stephanie changed the subject back to the disco ghost. "So, what do you need me to look up for you?"

Cheryl pushed her pad Thai around on her plate. "Anything you can find about the history of the building I live in would be good. And if you could find something about a tragedy that happened in a nightclub in the seventies here. What I keep seeing is a bunch of smoke slithering around the dance floor killing people. I'm not sure what that could represent, but I think there must have been a fire or something in the building. I also need to figure out who this ghost is. He's a dark-skinned man with an Afro. He's tall and broad. Could you see if you could figure out what his name is and his connection to the club? Maybe he died in the incident. Also, I keep seeing a woman with long dark hair and gold-colored leggings. She definitely died there too."

When Cheryl stopped talking, Stephanie was grinning from ear to ear. "This is so exciting. I feel like I'm a private investigator."

"Thanks for offering to help. If you can't find anything, don't worry about it. I'll figure something else out."

"I'm a great internet detective. I'll definitely find something."

Stephanie had been helpful before. Cheryl was happy to get any help resolving her latest ghost's problem so she could get this music out of her head.

During the meal, she kept her eye on the couple sitting at the table across the restaurant from them. She watched as they waited for their check to arrive.

"Maybe I should do something about this." She removed her napkin from her lap and put it down on the table. "I'll just be a minute," she told Stephanie before walking over to the couple's table. The little boy was next to her in no time, telling her how much he loved his parents. Cheryl wondered why she'd hesitated to approach them. Doing this was what she lived for. If only she could figure out how to help the ghost that kept playing music in her head. Hopefully, with Stephanie's assistance, she'd be able to figure out what he wanted soon.

***

Adam's niece and nephew, Carson and Chloe, were out on the front lawn before he got out of the car.

"Uncle Adam! Uncle Adam! Uncle Adam!" they chanted together as they jumped up and down in the grass.

Jules was close behind them, drying her hands on a checkered dishtowel. She flung the towel over her shoulder and walked over to hug him as he got out of the car. Her dark hair was pulled up into a messy bun. Wispy flyaways make a fuzzy halo around her head. She and Adam had very similar faces, strong jawlines and broad foreheads. People always immediately recognized that they were siblings.

"Look at the new car," she said in his ear as they hugged.

"It's nothing special." He turned to face the car with her. It really wasn't. The small silver SUV was the perfect car for his needs, but admittedly nothing that would turn heads. He liked it that way. He wasn't trying to get attention. He only needed something that would get the job done.

"A new car is always special. I need to get one." She nodded toward the beat-up white sedan he'd parked next to. "I'm driving that one into the ground."

Carson ran over, and Jules placed her hands on his shoulders. "How do you like Uncle Adam's new car?" She bent over, speaking into the top of his head.

He opened his eyes wide. "It looks like a spaceship." Then he pulled away from his mother to join his sister, running in circles on grass.

"I guess that's good," Jules said. She turned around to face the children, who laughed and looked up at the sky as they spun. Then they both collapsed into the grass in fits of laughter. Chloe rolled over before leaping to her feet and charging at Adam. She wrapped her arms around his legs with such force that he almost fell over. "You came for dinner!" she squealed.

"That I did." Adam rubbed her light-brown, curly hair. "Thanks for inviting me."

She pulled away from his legs and looked up at him, her dark eyes shining. "I can't invite you. Mom has to do that."

"Well, thanks for telling your mom to invite me."

She smiled, showing off a missing front tooth. "Sometimes Mom listens to me." She ran to the front door, her arms open wide like she was trying to fly.

"Dinner was delicious as usual." Adam wiped his face with a napkin.

Jules leaned over to rub the smattering of bright red spaghetti sauce from Carson's face. He wiggled and whined like she was hurting him. "Hold still," she said, holding his chin to check for any remaining red flecks. Then she looked over at Adam. "I'm glad you liked it. I figured you could use a home-cooked meal."

Adam glanced at the empty chair at the table. "Too bad Tim couldn't make it. It seems like ages since I've seen him."

"Yeah." Jules slumped in her seat. "He's been working late a lot. I hardly get to see him, and we live together."

Chloe wiped her mouth and got up from the table. "I want to show you something." She marched out of the room.

Adam gave Jules a questioning look.

Jules shrugged and raised an eyebrow.

Chloe spun around in the hallway, looking for Adam behind her. "Come on, Uncle Adam. It's important."

"Well, since it's important." He stood up. "I'll take care of the dishes in a minute. I have to go see whatever this is first. Clearly, it can't wait."

"Don't worry about the dishes. Carson's going to help me with them." Jules looked over at Carson, who nodded his head enthusiastically.

Chloe's bedroom was the color of sunshine. Watercolor paintings of horses running through fields and jumping over fences hung on the walls. Chloe sat on her yellow and white chevron rug with her legs crossed.

"What do you want to show me, munchkin?"

Adam only called her that because every time he did, she squealed with delight. She waved for him to come closer. He stepped into the room, his feet cushioned by the rug. He squatted, putting himself closer to eye level with her.

She got up and pushed the bedroom door closed. "There's someone in the house." She spoke in a loud whisper.

"Of course there is. We're all in the house."

She shook her head. "There's somebody in the house that's not supposed to be here." Her eyes widened as she raised her thread-thin eyebrows.

Adam looked around the room. "Really? Where?" He tried to sound unconcerned, but the air in the room had a new heaviness that disturbed him.

She looked around too, her movements exaggerated. Then she held a finger to her lips, shushing him. "He's just outside, and he doesn't like it when I talk about him."

Adam raised his gaze to the white door with Chloe's name written on it in swirling gray script. Chloe fell silent and turned to look at the door too. Anticipation gripped the air around them, and for a moment, Adam was convinced that someone sinister was standing just outside waiting to come in. The door flew open. Chloe yelled and jumped into Adam's arms.

Carson stood in the hallway, wiping his wet hands on his green T-shirt. "What are you doing?"

Relief rushed over Adam. He couldn't believe he'd let himself get so worked up.

"You scared me!" Chloe leaped up and ran toward her brother with her fist raised.

"Don't hit your brother." Adam stood, feeling a bit weak in his legs.

Chloe dropped her arm to her side and stuck out her tongue at Carson.

"Mom!" Carson yelled. "Chloe's being mean to me." He ran up the hallway on his little legs.

Adam and Chloe followed him up the hallway to the kitchen, where Jules was closing the dishwasher. "Chloe, you have to be nice to your brother," she said in a flat tone that reflected how many times she'd repeated the same words that day. When she stood up straight, Carson hid behind her peeking out at Adam and Chloe from behind his mother.

"Have you noticed anything strange happening around the house?" Adam asked Jules.

Chloe stomped her foot on the ground so hard her curls bounced. "It's a secret."

"I know. I'm not telling," Adam said to her.

Jules glanced down at her daughter. "What's a secret?"

"Nothing." Adam looked down at Chloe and winked before returning his attention to Jules. "I was wondering if you've noticed anything a bit off in the house."

He could tell by the way Jules looked at him that there was nothing. "Like what?" she asked.

"I don't know. I'm just asking." Adam didn't know if he'd really felt anything in Chloe's room or if it was all in his head. "If you do notice something, let me know."

A wry smile spread across Jules's face. "Do you think our house is—" She glanced at her children, not wanting to finish her sentence.

He knew what she was asking. "No." He'd been in this house so many times and had never seen anything out of the ordinary. "But if you do notice anything, make sure you call me. I wouldn't want anything to get out of hand here. The sooner you deal with it, the better."

"We've lived in this house forever. It's fine," she said.

"I know, but just in case something does happen, promise to call me." He looked down at Carson. His round face peeking out from behind his mother's hip.

"I promise." She held up her hands. "Enough with this. You're scaring the children."

"I'm not scared." Chloe crinkled her forehead.

"I'm not scared too." Carson stepped out from behind his mother with his hands on his hips.

Adam raised an eyebrow at his sister. "Maybe the only person I'm scaring is you."

Adam dropped the subject because he knew Jules didn't like talking about it. She still didn't know what to make of his new business or Cheryl. He hung around at his sister's house until it was time for the kids to go to bed. When he left, he sat in the car in the driveway for a few minutes, thinking. He hadn't seen anything unusual in the house, but something about it felt different. He hoped he was wrong.

Chapter 7

Cheryl's eyes flew open. The music was back. She rolled over and saw Adam lying on his side facing her. His eyelids were shut tight. He breathed the deep heavy breath of sleep. Cheryl sat up. Groping around on the floor, she found one of Adam's T-shirts and slipped it over her head. Then she padded into the living room. She stood in the darkness. She had to be alert, no matter how exhausted she felt. The music throbbed through her. The beat was so infectious she couldn't help but swing her hips just a little bit despite her fatigue. Then it happened. Everything around her melted away. The dance club was back, but this time no one danced. Bodies sprawled out on the shiny floor. She couldn't hear anything over the sound of the pumping disco beat. Cheryl froze with fear. She stood as still as a statue looking at the bodies, but then she remembered she couldn't afford to be shocked. She had to move. Her ghost was sending her this vision as a clue, and she had to figure out what he was trying to tell her. She took a deep breath and moved forward. This time instead of weaving through the crowd of dancers, she stepped over and around their bodies. She recognized one. The woman with the long black hair and the gold stretch pants lay in a heap on the floor. As she stared at her, Cheryl noticed that she was still alive. Her body heaved with each labored breath. The web of her dark hair had fallen in front of her face. Cheryl ran over to her.

"Are you okay?" It was a stupid question. She knew before she even asked it.

The woman wheezed and reached out a trembling hand. The hair fell from in front of her face revealing her glassy dark eyes. Her mouth moved as if she wanted to speak, but no sound came out. She took in one last lurching breath before the life slipped from her.

Cheryl looked up. In the shadows of the corridor across the dance floor, she saw her ghost, the man in black, dash onto the dancefloor with his back hunched, holding a piece of cloth over his mouth and nose. He froze, taking in the scene with the same horrified shock that Cheryl had. Dropping the cloth, he picked up the woman on the floor directly in front of him and put her over his shoulder. Then he disappeared out of sight up the back hallway. Cheryl was walking to the other side of the dance floor when he showed up again with the cloth over his face. He was yelling something that Cheryl couldn't quite make out. Cheryl rushed toward him. She needed to find out why he kept showing her this scene, but someone grabbed her. She yelped with surprise.

"Cheryl, wake up." Adam shook her.

She looked around and saw that she was standing in his living room. He had turned the lamp on, and it cast a soft yellow glow into the room. "I was at the disco again. This time everyone was dead, except the ghost in black. He wasn't responsible for whatever happened there. He looked just as surprised as I did when he saw that everyone was dead."

"But he still hasn't told you what he wants?" Adam asked, holding her arm.

"He hasn't told me anything yet. Hopefully, he will soon."

***

Janet woke up unusually early with a stiff neck and an aching shoulder from sleeping on the couch. The sun was just beginning to come up, casting a pinkish glow into the room through the sheers. She sat up and stretched.

She'd spent much of the night staring at the television with the sound muted and listening for unusual noises in the house. Unfortunately, there were too many for her to check out, so she pulled the green and white plaid throw blanket over her shoulders and hoped whatever she was hearing was only the house settling and not the thing that crawled out of the bathroom mirror. The long night had left her feeling tense and unrested. She stretched and made circles with her shoulders to loosen up her stiff muscles. Then she switched off the television and padded through the living room to peer in on Frank. He slept open-mouthed. His breathing rattled. He'd been quiet during the night, not stirring once.

Satisfied that he didn't need anything yet, she went to the kitchen to start a pot of coffee.

Silence bathed the neighborhood outside. Even the house was unusually quiet as Janet took the coffee can out of the cupboard and opened the lid. In the morning stillness, every sound she made seemed amplified: the crinkling of the coffee filters, the splashing of the water, the pop of the coffee can lid. She flipped the switch on the side of the coffeemaker with a click, and the red light lit up. It didn't take long before the water inside began to gurgle. As she stood and waited, she leaned her soft middle against the cool granite countertop with her back to the kitchen door, staring at the coffee maker.

Her mind was so tired. Each morning when she woke, she found herself hoping this would be the day nothing frightening would happen in the house. When did this strange life she was living creep up on her? She was pretty sure she hadn't lost her mind but wouldn't object to finding out that was the case all along. Finding out every strange thing that happened in the house was a figment of her imagination would be a welcomed discovery. That would be the simplest explanation. Too much had happened to explain any other way, the strange noises, Frank's creepy ramblings, the man in the mirror, the sludge coming out of the bathroom, and her general feeling of unease in the house.

The hairs on the back of Janet's neck stood on end. She took a deep breath, trying to calm her nerves. The coffee dripped steadily into the glass carafe. Janet felt like she wasn't in the kitchen alone. Someone was standing behind her. She was afraid of what she might see when she turned around. "Everything's okay. Everything's okay. There's no one else here." She repeated these words to herself, hoping to calm her pounding heart. An icy hand touched the small of her back. She inhaled sharply and whipped around to see the kitchen empty behind her.

"Frank?" she called out, convinced he had climbed out of his hospital bed and walked up behind her. She ran from the kitchen to his room and looked inside, where he still lay sleeping in the exact same position he was in before she started making the coffee. Her chest heaving, she went to his bedside. She was about to wake him when she realized the person lying in bed wasn't Frank at all. What lay in his bed wasn't even a person. Its eyes were on the side of its head like an insect. Instead of a nose, two tiny black holes sat in the middle of its face, and the mouth was one straight black line.

Janet dropped to her knees and let out a long, frightened scream. The room seemed to spin around her, and everything was out of control. The sound pouring out of her was all she could do to get rid of the stress. Then she heard her name.

"Janet! Janet, what's happening?" Frank was talking louder than he had spoken in a long time, but it was still drowned out by her screams. Eventually, she snapped out of it and looked up to see him white-knuckled holding the rail of the hospital bed, peering down at her, his eyes wide. It was her Frank, the real Frank, not the bug creature she had just seen.

Tears still streaming down her face, she said, "I came in here, and you weren't you. You were something else." She remained on the floor, sniffling and looking up at him. When she had slowed her breathing a bit and calmed down, she pushed herself to her feet. Exhausted, Frank lay back in his bed. She leaned over and kissed his head. "I came in here, and you were a bug or something. I don't know what you were, but you weren't human. It must have been a dream. It had to have been a dream. What else could it have been?" She ran her fingers across his bald head. "I was so scared."

He cut his eyes toward her. His expression was suddenly cold. "You should be afraid."

Janet gasped and looked down at her husband, who, to anyone else, would've looked like Frank, but the way the muscles at the corner of his lips twitched and his eyes seemed to slice through her to let her know that who she was looking at was not really Frank at all.

***

"Hey, Adam," Sofia squeezed Adam's shoulder as she went by.

Startled, he looked up to see her sauntering out into the

hallway in a tight, black, pencil skirt. Her shiny black hair hung straight down her back. "Hey," Adam said to her as she disappeared. His greeting came out sounding more like a question than a greeting.

She peered around the doorframe. "Drinks later?"

Adam shook his head. "I can't. I'm busy." He had been telling her that he was busy every time he'd been in the office now. She didn't seem to care though. He wondered when she would stop trying.

"Okay then. Next time." She raised her chin at him before disappearing again. He heard the clack of her heels going up the hallway.

"Jeez, man, I can't believe you just turned down drinks with Sofia." Ethan spun around in his chair to face Adam. His dark beard was speckled with gray. He wore a pair of round wire-framed glasses that looked like they came from a different era.

"I have a girlfriend. I told her that, but she just won't give up."

"Tenacious." He raised his eyebrows. "I wish I had your kind of problems." Ethan tapped his pen on his desk. "But I guess those are the kind of problems you have when you don't have a dad bod, and you've got that square movie star jawline. My chin is melting into my neck." He turned in his chair to give Adam a profile view of his face. He was indeed chinless. "Hence the beard."

"At least you can grow a beard. Mine is so patchy that it makes me look like a fifteen-year-old hobo."

Ethan chuckled before reaching up to stroke his beard as if he truly appreciated it now. "Maybe you should grow yours. Then Sofia will stop hitting on you."

"And my girlfriend would break up with me." He leaned back in his chair.

"How's the ghost business going?" The smirk on Ethan's face made Adam regret ever talking about Suncoast Paranormal.

Ethan was the only person he'd told about his new business venture, and he'd proceeded to tell everyone else in the office. He'd turned Adam into the butt of too many jokes. Since he'd started Suncoast Paranormal, he'd been given a Ghostbusters coffee mug, which he actually liked, a poster from the Ghostbusters reboot with the all-female cast, and more requests to exorcise people's haunted computers than he could count. It wasn't that bad really, but the fact that Ethan had such a big mouth still annoyed him. True, he'd never told him it was a secret but still.

"It's going good." He couldn't help but add a sharp edge to his voice when he talked about the business with Ethan.

"Is any of that stuff real? Do you think you're really finding ghosts and stuff?"

This was exactly why Adam didn't like talking about it. "Yup."

Ethan looked around as if to make sure they were the only ones in the room. "This might sound weird, but..." He looked over his shoulder again. Then he leaned in a bit closer and lowered his voice. "I was wondering if I could have your card. Something strange is going on with my mother, and I think..." He pressed his lips together and thought for a moment. "She says my father's been haunting her. At first, I thought it was senility. She is getting up there, you know? But now, my youngest daughter is saying weird things too. Granted, she's probably getting it from her grandmother, but maybe you and your girlfriend could come over to our house and take a look around. You could burn some candles and say some spells or whatever you do. That would calm things down in the house. It doesn't have to be real. They just have to think it's real, right?" He raised an eyebrow at Adam. "How much do you charge to do something like that?"

"I don't know about doing that. We're pretty slammed right now."

"You can't squeeze an old friend into your schedule. I'm sure it won't take long." He swiveled his chair back and forth.

Adam shook his head, suddenly feeling like he needed to leave. He pulled his cell from his pocket and checked the time. "I need to get over to human resources. Jay's been locked out of the company site all morning. I've got to take care of that before I head out for the day." He was already walking to the door.

"Right." Ethan pointed at him. "So, you'll call me then so you can take care of the problem with my mother?"

"Yeah, I'll call you." Adam hurried out the door.

He strolled up the bland gray hallway toward Jay's office. He was in no hurry to get there. This wasn't the first time Jay had this problem with the company website. It was always a quick fix. His phone vibrated in his pocket, and he pulled it out. He didn't immediately recognize the number but answered it just in case. "Suncoast Paranormal." He had finally made the decision to shift away from IT work and focus on their business. That meant most of the calls coming to his cell phone were about ghosts rather than broken computers.

"Hello." He immediately recognized her voice.

"Janet, how are you?" he asked.

"I know you're supposed to come this evening, but things in the house have been getting intense. I was hoping maybe you could move me up in your schedule, if you have any space at all." Her words were calm and measured. Adam and Cheryl had seen intense in their short time in the business, and this did not sound like a request from someone who was in the throes of a horrifying experience.

Adam stopped walking and leaned against the pale gray wall outside Jay's office. "When you say intense, what do you mean exactly?"

Janet lowered her voice as if she didn't want anyone else to hear and described everything that had happened that morning. Adam listened in silence, letting her finish before he said anything.

"So, how is Frank now? Do you still think he isn't really your husband?" he asked.

Her voice broke, but she tried to hide it by clearing her throat again. "No. He's different. I can see it in his eyes. I know his eyes, and the man in the hospital bed isn't my Frank." She let out a sob.

"I can come over for a few minutes this afternoon to check things out if you like." He knew Cheryl's schedule was packed for the day, but that didn't stop him from going over himself.

"Please. That would be such a comfort to me." Her relief was palpable.

"I'll see you soon."

"Thank you so much. See you later."

Adam felt a certain measure of relief too. The business had actually been moving fast, faster than he'd ever imagined it would. They were picking up new clients all the time now. Even people he would never suspect would be interested in their services, like Ethan, asked them to go to their houses to do cleansing rituals. Those weren't things Adam knew anything about, but Cheryl did. He was happy to tag along and learn. This work brought out the best in him, and he was constantly trying to figure out how to get more of it. So, it didn't matter that Cheryl couldn't be there. He was more than happy to go on his own, even if all he was doing was providing comfort to a woman who was struggling. He already knew Janet's case was so much more than that though. He just hoped Frank wasn't really possessed because possession added complications to any case and the last thing they needed was more complications.

Chapter 8

"Sorry I'm late," Cheryl said as she rushed into Day's store.

"Don't apologize to me. Apologize to your client. She's waiting in the back." Day pointed to the back corner of the store where Cheryl did her readings. "If you didn't show up soon, I was going to go back there and give her a reading myself."

Day and Cheryl were friends, but Cheryl's tardiness was definitely bad for business. She'd gotten all wrapped up in one of her calls for the hotline, and it had ended up going much longer than she expected. When it was over, she collapsed on the couch to close her eyes for a few minutes but somehow she'd drifted off to sleep. She awoke to Beau standing on her chest, staring into her face with his inquisitive green eyes.

She hurried past Day to the back of the store. "I'm so sorry. My reading with another client ran late, and..." She rounded the screen that separated her work area from the rest of the store, and her mouth dropped open. She couldn't believe who was sitting there. Day had made this appointment for her, and Cheryl had not seen or spoken to the client in advance. Even if she had only talked to her on the phone, she was sure she would have recognized her. "Connie."

Connie was the former owner of the Starlight Café. Cheryl had stopped reading tarot cards there after Connie had basically kicked her out. She'd accused her of stealing drinks, but it was all just a misunderstanding. Day knew the whole story. Why would she book an appointment with her without telling Cheryl who she was seeing in advance?

"I was starting to think you weren't going to show up." Connie looked up at her with her pale round face. The combination of her light blue eyes and short gray hair gave her a ghostly appearance.

"I don't stand my clients up." Cheryl didn't want to read Connie's cards, but a client was a client, and she needed all the clients she could get. She sat down in the old wooden chair on the other side of the table. It was a bit wobbly. Day had said she would fix it but hadn't gotten around to it yet. Cheryl smoothed the black tablecloth in front of her. A smattering of golden stars decorated the dark fabric. She pulled her favorite tarot deck from her purse without saying another word. She gingerly removed the cards from the purple velvet pouch she carried them in and placed them on the table. Then she twisted around to the shelf behind her and mumbled a prayer to herself before lighting the candles and a stick of sandalwood incense. She took the cards and held them in the smoke of the incense to cleanse them before starting the reading. She did all this without saying a word to Connie. When she turned back around to face her, Connie was staring at her. The mixture of anger and humiliation Cheryl felt kept her from looking into Connie's face for too long. When Connie told her she couldn't read at the cafe anymore, she'd lost quite a bit of income. It had been one of the main places she'd worked. Cheryl wasn't a good businesswoman. She was all too aware of that. She hadn't collected the names and numbers of the clients she saw there. She had no way of letting any of them know where to find her, so half of her client base dropped away. She couldn't blame Connie for her financial troubles though. She was in trouble long before that happened, but it didn't help.

She cut the deck and shuffled it a few times. Then she stacked it on the table between them. "So, Connie." She tried to keep her name soft and round as she said it, concealing any lingering resentment. "Why did you come for a reading today? Is there a specific question you have for the deck?"

Connie's left eye twitched ever so slightly. "I was hoping things wouldn't be weird between us. I'm looking for some answers, and you're the only tarot reader I know."

"Nothing's weird here." That was clearly a lie. "You don't have to know the person to get your cards read by them." Cheryl stated the obvious.

"You're probably right, but I feel more comfortable dealing with someone I know. Besides, you're the one who predicted that I'd meet Lenny in the first place." Her gaze drifted down to the deck of cards.

Cheryl remembered the reading. Back then she mostly told her clients what they wanted to hear. Connie needed to find love at the time. It was obvious to everyone but her that she felt desperately alone. So, Cheryl told her she would meet the man of her dreams, and she had. Most of the time people only needed a suggestion that something would happen in their lives to nudge them in that direction. Cheryl hadn't predicted anything really. She'd only given Connie permission to let love in. Once she was in a better state of mind, love naturally found her.

Cheryl took a deep breath and placed her hands on the table. She had another client scheduled to come in after Connie, so she needed to get the reading underway. "So what's your question?"

"I just came back from a trip with my boyfriend. It was an Alaskan cruise. I'd always wanted to go on one, and it was truly amazing. If you ever get the chance to go, you really should." Her eyes sparkled.

Cheryl listened in disbelief. Was she really going to sit there and tell her about her cruise and not once apologize for accusing her of stealing? "That's nice. So, what's your question for the deck?" Some clients had to be prompted to get to the point multiple times before they did. Usually, Cheryl was happy to hear their stories, but she wasn't interested in Connie's.

"Well, my boyfriend is great. He's creative and well off and says all the right things. The trip was amazing, but for some reason, the whole time, I felt like things were a bit off between us. I kept waiting for the other shoe to drop, if you know what I mean?"

Cheryl knew exactly what she meant. Unfortunately, whenever she'd had that feeling in her own life, it had been true. The other shoe would always drop eventually. When it did, it was as loud and heavy as an anchor. "So, you don't think he is who he says he is?"

Connie gave a curt nod.

"So, you want to know about your love life?" She pushed the cards across the table at Connie. "Think about the specific question you have for the deck and give the cards a shuffle." Cheryl's heart softened. While she'd never quite felt like things in her own life were too good to be true, she could understand the uneasiness that feeling might instill.

Connie shuffled the deck clumsily. She certainly didn't have a future as a card shark. One card flew out of the deck, landing on the floor. Connie's face grew flush with embarrassment, and Cheryl felt even more pity for her. She reached down to pick up the card and set it to the side. "This one has something special to say to you. We'll look at it later." She took the deck from Connie and straightened it before pushing it back toward her again. "Cut it into three piles."

"Even piles?" Connie asked.

"Even, uneven, whatever you want. You cut it where it feels good to you." In this situation, some people become childlike. They wanted so badly to please her by doing the right thing. Connie was one of those people. When she told Cheryl that she wasn't welcome to do her readings at the Starlight Café anymore, she'd seemed like she'd had so much power and control. There she was, telling Cheryl what she could and couldn't do. She'd had no interest in discussing the matter. She offered no empathy or understanding. As she sat in front of Cheryl now, she looked lost. Cheryl realized that the only reason anything Connie had done had power over her was because she'd let it. She had gotten so used to being a victim that she put herself in that position by default. She needed to stop doing that, but she wasn't sure how.

Connie carefully separated the cards into three piles. Then she looked up at Cheryl for approval. Cheryl smiled and nodded her head.

"Now choose a pile. Take your time and choose one that feels right."

Connie looked down at the cards. She hovered her hand over the pile on her left for a few moments before changing her mind and picking the middle stack of cards. This stack was small, containing only a few cards. Cheryl knew before even taking the pile in her hand there weren't enough for the type of reading she usually did, but Connie needed something different. She set the other cards to the side. "Your question is about this man that you're dating, is that right?"

Connie nodded earnestly. Cheryl examined her. She always

watched to see what else her clients were telling her with their body language. People had a myriad of ways of communicating with each other. Words were only the smallest bit.

"You want to know if he is lying to you, correct?"

Connie parted her lips slightly and then pressed them together.

"Go on. Say whatever it is you were getting ready to say just then." Cheryl was sure to keep her voice calm and steady.

"I really want it to work out. It's just that I've been alone since Marty..." Her words trailed off.

She didn't have to tell Cheryl her story because Cheryl already knew. Connie had dedicated much of her life to her husband, a sculptor and an alcoholic. She stayed with him until she couldn't anymore. She'd always acted so cavalier when she talked about their split. Connie invested a lot of energy in appearing strong, but she was as tender as a fresh wound beneath her tough exterior.

Cheryl nodded to let her know she understood. She laid the cards out on the table in a neat line.

Since Cheryl had started seeing ghosts, her connection with the dead wasn't the only thing that had changed in her life. Seeing what most people could not opened her to the idea that this world and life itself was much bigger than she had previously known. That changed the way she saw tarot and her whole relationship to being a tarot reader. What she had previously treated as a kind of coaching session for her clients had become something else entirely. She no longer depended on her own knowledge. Now the words she spoke seemed to come from someplace else. She trusted the cards in a way that she hadn't before. Words flowed from her lips. She told Connie a story of love and happiness that she would not have had the courage to predict if she was speaking from what she knew of the world. How could she promise someone else something that she didn't believe in herself? That hurt her heart, but belief could be hard to change. She didn't look at Connie's face as she spoke. Instead, she looked down at the cards, and when she nearly finished, she reached over to the card that had fallen on the floor and turned it over. She held it up to Connie, telling her that meant more good news. When she was finished, she looked into Connie's eyes. Tears streamed down her cheeks. She reached into her pocket and pulled out an old, crumpled tissue and wiped her eyes. "That's better news than I could've imagined."

Cheryl swallowed and looked down at the cards again. Their lovely bright colors told a clearer story than anything she could have made up herself. "It is, isn't it." Tarot had been her gateway into this strange and magical life she was living, and it would always be her home.

Connie reached across the table and squeezed Cheryl's hand. "Thank you. Thank you so much."

"Don't thank me. Thank the cards." Feeling slightly embarrassed, Cheryl gathered up the cards and avoided Connie's eyes.

Connie gave her a twenty-dollar tip on top of the normal reading fee.

As Cheryl tidied up and waited for her next client, Day came around the screen to talk to her. "That must have gone well. She practically floated out of here."

Cheryl smiled. "Surprisingly, it did."

"What do you mean by surprisingly?" Day picked up the deck and shuffled it.

"I haven't talked to her since she asked me to stop reading in the Starlight Café."

Day took in a sharp breath. She held a hand to her chest. "I'm sorry. I forgot all about that. I would've never booked her if I had remembered." She fanned the cards out on the table in front of Cheryl.

"Don't worry about it. It's good that she came. I needed to talk to her and release all of the resentment I was still feeling."

"Think about a question and make a choice." Day motioned to the cards.

Cheryl closed her eyes and focused her energy on finding an answer to her financial woes. Then she chose a card from the table and handed it to Day without looking at it.

"No grudges?" Day remained stone faced as she looked at the card.

"No grudges."

"That's what I like to hear. You're on your way to something big, but first, you'll have to let some things go." Day turned the card in her hand to face Cheryl to reveal a building tumbling to the ground. Bolts of lightning cracked in the sky around it. People dove from its windows to their deaths.

A puff of air escaped Cheryl's nose. "The Tower."

"Don't look so sad. You need a change right now. Sometimes everything has to come crashing to the ground to make that happen." A chime sounded announcing the arrival of a new customer. Day placed the card face up on the table. "It will be all right. The Universe knows exactly what you need." She smiled before walking around the divider. "Welcome," she said to the customer.

Cheryl sat still as a stone, looking down at the card on the table. If upheaval was what she needed, she'd be able to deal with it. Her entire life had been a series of upheavals until now. She placed her hand on the card. "Bring it on," she whispered. "I'm ready."

Chapter 9

Janet answered the door with her eyes rimmed in red from crying. "I'm so glad you came." She held out a hand to Adam, welcoming him into the house. He noticed the dark, heavy feeling as soon as he stepped inside. It was different from the last time he was there.

"No problem. It's important that I check out everything as close to the time it happened as possible. Thank you for calling me." He noticed one of his cameras set up on the tripod in the living room. He'd tucked it back into a corner to keep it out of the way.

Janet turned to see what he was looking at. "Do you think it captured anything?" Her eyes grew wide.

"I don't know. Let's hope so."

Janet watched him silently.

Her expectations weighed on him. "So, it happened in the kitchen?" He looked through the living room to the arched doorway that led to the kitchen.

"Yes." Janet pulled her gray cardigan tight across her frame. The air in the house was stagnant and much too warm for a sweater. Noticing him looking at her, she crossed her arms over her chest. "I've had a chill I can't seem to shake ever since what happened this morning. I even went out in the backyard to sit in the sun and warm up, but it didn't seem to help."

He followed her through the cramped living room to the kitchen. Once he stepped through the arched doorway, the temperature dropped ten degrees. The hairs rose on his arms. "There's definitely something going on in here."

"You don't have to tell me." Janet walked over to the counter by the sink where the coffee maker still sat plugged in. "I was right here when it happened." She patted the tile countertop. "There was a hand on my back. It was cold as ice just like I told you. Then I turned around, and no one was there. Now every time I come in here, I get a weird feeling. It's like somebody is in here with me."

Adam nodded. "I can feel it too." He walked over to the camera he'd placed near the refrigerator. The wide-angle lens was positioned to get the entire kitchen into frame. "Let's look at this and see if we got anything." He took the camera from the tripod and began scrolling through the videos. "About what time did this happen?"

"It was seven. I always put the coffee on at seven." She looked down at the floor for a moment. "I didn't call you right away. I thought it would be too early, and it took me a while to process what had happened."

"That's okay." He looked over at her.

Deep worry lines creased her forehead. She slouched, and with her arms crossed like they were, she had the appearance of someone clinging to themselves for safety. She nodded. "I should always make sure I call you as soon as I can, right? I mean, I don't want them to get away before you get here."

Adam chuckled. "It doesn't quite work like that." He scrolled through videos looking for the one from that morning. When he found it, he pressed Play. Janet stood close to him so she could see the screen.

"Yep. There I am. I hate watching videos of myself." She sighed as if resigned to the torture of watching her image on the tiny screen.

Adam focused on the video. She prepared the coffee maker methodically like it was a kind of ritual for her. Once she was done, she stood with her belly leaning against the counter, looking down at the coffee pot. Suddenly she jumped and turned around. She said something. Then she left the room.

She brought her hand to her mouth and chewed on the skin on the side of her thumb. "There was something there. I swear there was something there."

"Don't worry. I believe you." There was nothing visible in the video, but that didn't mean there was nothing there. "Well, it definitely wasn't your husband."

Janet still looked at the screen. "I guess it wasn't. Unless he can somehow make himself invisible now." She laughed dryly. "Maybe that's a side effect of cancer."

Adam returned the camera to the tripod. "I'm going to keep this in here in case something else happens." He looked around the room. "Is there anything unusual you remember happening before you felt the hand on your back?"

She raised her hand to her chin and put on a pensive expression. "No. It was a normal morning. Well, as normal as any morning has been recently." Janet nodded sincerely.

Adam pulled the EMF meter out of his pocket and turned it on.

"What's that?" Janet asked, craning her neck to see the display as the gadget sprang to life.

"It's an EMF meter. I'm just going to walk around the kitchen with it and see if it picks up any unusual activity."

Adam liked to be organized as he used the meter. He went to the far corner of the kitchen holding the gadget out in front of him to see the screen and began to walk the kitchen, checking the readings. Part of him doubted the EMF meter really worked at all because he was yet to be successful finding any paranormal activity with it, but he was still learning.

"So that thing will tell you if there's a ghost in here?" Janet sounded just as doubtful as he felt.

"It will let us know if there's any unusual activity in the room." As he walked the kitchen, the only place it spiked was near the refrigerator, but that was to be expected.

Janet watched him the whole time, scowling. When he got to the last area of the kitchen near the door, she asked, "Anything?" Her voice was tight with anxiety.

Adam shook his head.

"Maybe you should check the rest of the house." She motioned toward the arched kitchen doorway. "I think that would help."

Adam stepped out of the kitchen into the short hallway that led to the stairs. "I'll start upstairs and work my way down." He looked back at Janet, who was trailing behind him.

"That's a good idea. Maybe you should start in the bathroom."

As they went along the short hall to the stairs, they passed the bedroom where Frank lay in his hospital bed. The door was cracked, and as they approached, Adam saw Frank sit up in bed, his back ramrod straight. He turned his head to face the door and Adam swore his eyes gleamed red. "Did you see that?" he asked Janet who had to double back to look in the door too. Maybe she was right and Frank was possessed.

"What?" she asked.

Adam looked down at the EMF meter. The readings spiked. He brought it closer to the bedroom door, and the needle continued to rise.

"What's that mean?" Janet asked, looking at the screen.

The reading could've been from something electrical in Frank's room, or it could've been something else, something none of them could see. Adam grabbed the door and flung it open.

The nurse, Yvette, looked up, shocked. "What are you doing?"

Adam walked into the room, holding the meter out in front of him. Frank's mouth opened impossibly wide and he let out a roar. Yvette looked at him with wide eyes. "What's wrong?" she asked, trying her best to maintain her professional calm. She walked over to Frank, who roared at her again. His mouth was open so wide that his jaw cracked, and the corners of his mouth began to split. He twisted his head violently back and forth. "Are you in pain?" She went to the cart at the end of the room and began preparing a syringe with shaky hands. It took longer than usual for her to remove the needle from its wrapper. Her fingers didn't seem to want to work. Adam and Janet stood frozen in the doorway, neither knowing what to do.

Yvette spun around with the syringe in her hand. Then Frank fell back on the bed, his body limp. All three of them rushed over to him. He lay with his eyes closed. His breath heavy as if he were sleeping. The jagged red splits at the corners of his mouth didn't seem nearly as large as they looked when he was sitting up. They only looked to be the result of very dry lips.

Janet shook him awake. "Frank, Frank."

He blinked his heavy lids open. "Yes," he whispered.

"Are you okay?"

He looked around the room puzzled. His gaze fell on each of their faces before answering. "As okay as I can be?"

Yvette returned the syringe to the tray and let out a sigh, releasing the tension from her body. "You gave us a scare."

"What did I do?" He raised his head to look at her.

"You were screaming like someone was stabbing you." Yvette waved her hand in front of her face like she was too hot. "Do you mind if I go outside and smoke for a couple of minutes to calm my nerves?" She was already pulling a pack of cigarettes from her pocket before Janet had even answered.

Janet nodded. "Go on, Yvette. We all need a break after that."

She brushed past Adam on the way out the door. He turned off the EMF meter and put it back into his pocket. He didn't need the constant flashing light to know something was in this room. They'd all seen it. Tension gripped his throat, making it difficult to breathe. He walked over to the hospital bed. "Hello, Frank."

Frank's eyelids fluttered, and he lowered his chin just enough to indicate that he heard Adam. Adam noticed bright red scratches on his bare arms and a pink welt rising on the pale skin above his collarbone.

"Nice to meet you. My name is Adam. Your wife hired me because there have been some strange things going on around the house."

Frank raised his eyebrows slightly, and his gaze drifted to Janet.

She yanked at the edges of her cardigan, pulling it tightly around her, and stepped forward. Then she reached out and gingerly placed her hand on his. "I know you don't believe in this kind of stuff, Frankie, but some crazy things have been happening. I haven't told you because... well," she choked back a sob.

Frank's face was unmoving. He looked at her through large round eyes.

"I didn't want to upset you, but there's something evil in this house." Her voice broke.

A sly grin slid across Frank's face. "Evil? What is evil?" he croaked. His eyes flashed red again.

Janet pulled her hand from his and held it over her open mouth.

Suddenly the façade around them dropped away, and Adam's vision was clear. A swirling black hole opened above the hospital bed. Hordes of skeletal beings danced around the black hole with gaping empty sockets for eyes and mouths open in an eternal scream. Just as quickly as the scene showed itself to Adam, it vanished.

"Frank," Janet said. "What's wrong with your eyes?" She backed away from him.

"Nothing, Janet. Nothing at all. What's wrong with you?" His sinister smile cracked his chapped bottom lip revealing the dewy pink flesh beneath the skin.

Janet reached out, taking hold of the doorframe to steady herself. "You're not Frank."

He twisted his head to get a better look at her standing across the room. "Are you sure?"

Adam stepped in front of him, blocking his view of Janet. "What are you? What have you done with Frank?" He put power behind his voice.

Frank blinked a few times, and a blank expression came across his face. "What's happening?"

"Frank?" Janet went around Adam, returning to Frank's bedside. "Is that you?"

"Of course it's me. Who else would I be?" He looked down, a hint of concern on his face.

"You're possessed." Adam stepped forward.

"Who are you?" Frank looked from Janet to Adam.

"He's one of the people I called to help deal with all the

strange stuff going on here recently. Remember?" She pulled a tissue from her pocket and wiped her nose.

He reached out and took hold of her hand. "I know. There's something evil in the house. We have to do something about it because it will only get worse."

"Do you know what it is?" Adam asked.

Frank shook his head. "No, but I do know it's dangerous, and I think it's here because of me."

"Frank, no," Janet objected, squeezing his hand. "This has nothing to do with you."

Adam ignored her objections. "What do you mean by that?"

Frank began blinking rapidly. His eyelids suddenly heavy. "I'm sorry. I..." He closed his eyes completely for a few seconds. It was a struggle to open them again, but he managed to do it. His voice was only a whisper as he said, "I called a demon out. It's all my fault." He closed his eyes.

"Frank." Janet shook his shoulder.

His eyes opened, just barely. "The book," he whispered. "I didn't..." He closed his eyes again and drifted off to sleep. His breathing deepened.

"Frank, wake up." Janet shook his shoulder.

His head lolled to the side.

Yvette came back in smelling of cigarette smoke. She paused at the door, and upon seeing how Janet was shaking Frank trying to wake him, asked, "What's wrong?"

"I don't know. He was talking and suddenly he passed out," Janet said.

Adam stepped to the side to let Yvette get to Frank more easily. Yvette walked over to the bed side and Frank began to snore. "It looks like he just fell asleep to me."

"But I can't wake him," Janet said.

"He needs his rest," Yvette said.

Janet looked at Adam who nodded. "I'm going to look around the rest of the house." He went to the door and Janet followed him reluctantly. They went upstairs, and once Janet thought they were out of Yvette's earshot, she spoke to Adam in a loud whisper. "What do you think he meant when he said he let a demon in?"

"He must've done something to unleash some kind of negative force here. Can you think of anything he might've done?"

She shook her head. "I don't know. That's not the type of thing Frank would mess with or even believe in."

"Sometimes not believing is what gets you in trouble." He looked down the hallway. He didn't need his EMF meter to see what was wrong up here. "What's that?" He pointed at the thick black sludge oozing from under the bathroom door.

Janet's worried expression transformed into a wide smile. She spun around and wrapped her arms around Adam, hugging him tight. Then she let go and pointed at the goo seeping beneath the bathroom door. "I can't believe you can see it too! I'm not crazy. I called a plumber this morning, and he didn't see anything. I tried to show it to Yvette, and she couldn't see it either."

There was pure evil in the room. Adam knew it. He felt it more strongly now than he had ever felt a presence in the past. "Let's go outside and talk for a minute." He couldn't be in there any longer. He needed some air.

He followed Janet down the stairs and straight out the front door. She fell to her knees, crying on the front lawn, and Adam wished Cheryl was there.

"How could this happen? I don't understand," she repeated.

Adam spoke in a calm even tone until she calmed down. He helped her to her feet.

"What am I supposed to do now?" she asked, wiping her eyes.

Adam looked at the house. He wasn't sure what to tell her. He needed Cheryl. "Go back inside and act normal."

She took a deep breath and looked at the door. "Okay. Then what?"

"I'm going to get my partner and come back later to deal with this, but I need you to hold on a bit longer."

She nodded. "I can do that. I have to for Frank, right?"

"Yes."

"Okay."

Adam felt bad about sending her back in the house alone, but she'd been there all this time. He watched her go inside before getting in his car. He needed to find Cheryl.

Chapter 10

Cheryl walked up the sidewalk toward her apartment building. Her reading with Connie lingered in her thoughts. People's perceptions were so different. Connie didn't even seem to register that what she had done hurt her. Cheryl was shocked because to her it seemed so obvious.

It had been a good afternoon for doing readings at Day's shop. Day had her booked solid for the entire four hours she was there. That wasn't what she was expecting, and goodness knows she needed the cash. Too bad it wouldn't stay in her bank account long. Not having money made her think about it more than she ever had before.

It was early. Only five o'clock in the evening. She had enough time to relax before she started her late shift on the psychic network. She'd been snapping up as many shifts as she could these days. But it seemed like her bank account was a black hole.

Cheryl walked by the grocery store where homeless people hung out on the benches at the bus stop. She wondered what it would be like to sleep there. These days she was starting to feel like that could be a real possibility for her. Fortunately, she wasn't behind on her rent yet.

A man hobbled up to her. His shirt looked like it might've been white once, but now it was a dingy gray. A long belt held up his soiled oversized jeans. The end of the belt hung awkwardly around his thighs. "Pardon me, ma'am. Do you have a dollar? I need to go inside and get something to eat." He motioned to the grocery store.

Cheryl was never quite sure what to do in the situation, but because there were so many people around, she thought it was probably safe, so she stopped. She reached into her purse and, without pulling her wallet from her bag, opened it and got a dollar. "Here you go." She handed it to the man. She knew if she ever ended up in that situation herself, she would be so grateful for anyone who would offer her help. She had been homeless when she left Mark. And she wasn't that far away from it now.

"Thank you, and God bless you." The man held his hands together as if praying and bowed his head.

His gratitude embarrassed her. "No problem." Her phone beeped in her purse. Hurrying away from the man, she reached inside and pulled it out. It was a text from Adam.

Adam: Something happened at Janet's today. I need your help. Can you work tonight?

She was hoping to get a little bit of rest before she started her late shift on the hotline. She had felt lucky to get two shifts in one day, but no matter how exhausted she felt, she knew Adam wouldn't be texting her for help if it wasn't something serious.

Cheryl: Sure. Let me feed Beau and myself, and then I'll go over there with you.

This evening was going to be anything but restful.

**

Janet leaned her back against the front door and listened as Yvette walked down the walkway to her car parked on the side of the road. The engine started with a cough, then the car pulled away from the curb, leaving Janet and Frank alone.

She took a deep breath before turning and locking the door, an act that felt more like it was trapping herself in than keeping bad people out these days. The house was painfully quiet. She couldn't even hear Frank snoring in the next room. She went into the living room, where the curtains on the many windows stood open. The sun was low in the sky. She wondered how long it would be before the paranormal investigators came back.

She grabbed the remote control and turned on the television as a distraction. It didn't matter what was on, just as long as she didn't have to a listen to the silence. The drone of the television made her feel less alone. She settled into the sofa in front of the news. The gray-haired anchorman talked about a murder-suicide that had happened that morning. It was not the type of story she wanted to hear. She was about to change the channel when she thought she heard something coming from Frank's room. A low gravelly moan floated through the air. Janet muted the television and listened. It was silent again. She unmuted the television, and the anchorman continued to talk. The moan happened again. She turned off the television and listened.

Silence.

The sofa creaked as she stood, still holding the remote control in her hand. "Frank, are you okay?" She spoke into the empty air. The soft surfaces in the room absorbed her voice.

Silence answered her.

Janet considered turning the television back on and sitting on the sofa. She was only hearing things. That must have been it. Just as she'd convinced herself she hadn't heard anything, the sound rumbled through the air again. She put down the remote and walked through the living room to the back hallway.

A pungent sulfur scent greeted her when she entered the hallway. She gagged and put her hand over her mouth and nose before creeping to Frank's room.

"What's that smell?" she whispered to herself.

Frank lay in bed on his side with his back facing her. A mint-green knitted blanket was pulled up over his shoulders, and his head was bent toward his chest, revealing the bumps of his cervical vertebrae above the collar of his loose-fitting pajamas.

The light in the room gave everything a blue tinge. "Frank, are you asleep?" she whispered into the cup of her hand as she stepped inside the room. She waited.

Sometimes the dim light can play tricks on the eyes. That's why Janet wasn't completely sure what she saw, but she thought she saw something wriggling beneath the skin of his neck like worms slithering between his vertebrae. The long, tapered shapes squirmed under his skin. Janet's eyes grew wide. She approached his bedside quietly, the soft carpet cushioning her footfall.

She leaned over to get a closer look at his neck. Could this be a result of his illness? She reached out a tentative finger to touch his graying skin when he rolled over, whipping his head around to face her.

Sometimes someone may look like the person you know. They might have the same eyes, nose, and mouth. Everything about their face and their body may be configured in the exact right way, but you know something's wrong. Something was terribly wrong, and Janet knew it when Frank rolled over and looked at her. Pure hatred filled his eyes and his face twisted into a snarl.

Janet snatched her hand away from the bed. "Frank?" Her voice quivered.

He reached out his bony hand and caught her arm. Then he growled at her, showing his yellowing teeth. Saliva dripped from his mouth down his chin. He pulled her arm into him. His mouth opened wide like he was planning to bite a chunk from her flesh.

"No!" Janet yelled, trying to work her arm free, but he was much stronger than he should have been. She twisted her arm this way and that and was finally able to break free. As she did, she fell backward on the floor, jarring her spine as she hit the ground. Shaken, she sat there crying loudly. The whole world around her became a blur of tears. She wiped them away and was ready to flee, but when she found her way to her feet, she looked over and saw he was lying on his back. His mouth was slightly open, and he slept deeply. His arms were tucked beneath his blanket in such a manner that it would've been impossible for him to reposition himself like that.

Janet looked at her own arm. Her flesh still throbbed in the place where he had grabbed her. The skin was marked in red. What was happening? Was she losing her mind?

She sniffled and was ready to turn and leave the room when Frank stirred. He blinked a few slow, long blinks. "There you are, baby doll." His voice was raspy with sleep.

Hearing him call her by his nickname for her made the tears roll down her face again. His forehead creased. "I don't want you to worry, darling."

"I don't want to worry." She smiled weakly. It had been so long since she had seen traces of who her husband used to be. "It's been so hard." She felt like she should approach his bed again, but fear held her back, urging her to keep her distance just in case.

"I know." His words slurred together in a groggy haze. "But when we're together, nothing can stop us." He blinked lazily, his eyelids drooping.

"Earlier today you were telling me something about a demon. You said you called it. Do you remember? I really need to know what you meant."

He creased his forehead and looked away from her for a moment. He parted his pale lips as if he was about to say something and then pulled them together again.

"What is it, Frank? You can tell me."

He turned his gaze to the ceiling and his eyes grew wide with fright.

"Frank, what is it? What's wrong?" She looked up but only saw the smooth white plaster overhead.

"Forget it. It's best you forget everything I said."

"What do you mean, forget it? Something is going on in this house. I can't forget it. It's driving me crazy." Her voice rose and tears pricked the back of her eyes.

"You're just under a lot of pressure, so you're making things up. I don't blame you. This would be a lot for anyone. It's going to be okay, Janet." He reached out to take her hand, but she pulled it away.

"What are you saying? You know what I'm talking about. Don't pretend it's not happening."

"It will all be over soon." He closed his eyes and took a deep breath.

"What do you mean by that?" She watched his unmoving face.

He sighed and his eyes remained closed. "I'm sorry," he said. "I love you." His breathing deepened. And he returned to the world of sleep.

A soup of emotions swirled around inside Janet. What was he sorry for, and how could she stop what was happening? She didn't know the answers, but she hoped Adam and Cheryl would give them to her, so she and Frank could spend his last days in this life in peace.

Chapter 11

"I'm so glad you came back." Janet looked wearier than she had when Adam had been there earlier that day.

"How's it been here?" Adam and Cheryl stepped inside the narrow, dark entryway. The walls, covered in deep brown wood paneling, felt like they were closing in on them.

"Okay, I guess." Her voice quivered. "I can't even begin to tell you how glad I am you're here." She looked from Cheryl to Adam. "It's been so much." Her voice caught, and she put her hand to her chest.

"How's Frank doing? Can I take a look in his room?" Cheryl asked.

"Of course."

Cheryl walked into the room where Frank slept. Even though she always told Adam she didn't really know what she was doing, she looked so confident in these situations. She stood at Frank's bedside, looking down at the sleeping man. His face was angled slightly upward, exposing the crepe-like skin on his neck.

Janet stood next to Adam in the doorway, watching Cheryl.

"What's she going to do?" she whispered to Adam.

Adam shrugged. He felt like he was never quite sure what Cheryl would do in these situations.

Cheryl leaned over the bed, so her face was close to Frank's. The bangles on her wrist clacked together. She stayed there for a moment. Something on the other side of the bed caught her attention. She jerked her head up, staring at the wall. Then she stood up.

"Hello," she said into the air.

"Who is she talking to?" Janet whispered.

Adam didn't answer. Instead, he looked at the space that Cheryl spoke into, hoping to see something too.

***

Dying people have a smell. Pungent and dark, it lingered in the air. Cheryl couldn't help but feel sympathy for the man lying before her. It was at times like these when people are most vulnerable to malevolent spirits lurking around us. She leaned over Frank, getting a close look at him: the way his greenish veins showed prominently through his skin; his cracked lips; the yellowing spots on his temples. She wondered what he looked like before all of this. She could still see the shadow of the man he once was behind the veil of impending death.

Something uninvited lingered in the room just beyond the edges of her senses. She couldn't see it or feel it, but she felt how it took up space. She looked down at Frank's hands, resting on his stomach. They moved up and down slowly with his breath.

The ghost materialized on the other side of Frank's bed. His stare made her look up. A man stood opposite her. She'd seen him before. He was so tall his head nearly hit the ceiling. His pale, narrow face was placid and still. He wore a dark suit with a white shirt, the top two buttons open at the neck with no tie. His long arms hung at his sides. She stood upright.

Cheryl was not afraid. She didn't even jump when she saw him. Instead, she greeted him like he was supposed to be there.

"Hello."

He blinked at her as if surprised.

"Who are you?" she asked. She could hear Janet and Adam talking to each other in hushed tones behind her, but she focused her attention on the man standing on the other side of the bed.

He drew his eyebrows together but didn't answer her.

"I'm Cheryl." She looked down at Frank lying in his bed. "I'm here to help him." She looked back up at the man standing across from her. "What's your name? What do you want?" She made sure her voice was friendly and inviting. She wanted to let him know she was there to help him.

The man angled his face upward, looking at the ceiling. Following his lead, Cheryl did too, and she saw a hole open up above them. The ceiling melted away, exposing a gaping dark hole, swirling with wispy skeletal creatures. They spun in circles and danced around one another in an eerie celebration. Their frightful faces split nearly in half by wide mouths full of pointy teeth.

She swallowed the fear rising in her throat. Then she twisted around to look at Adam, who was looking up too, and she knew by the look on his face that he saw what she saw too. "This is what you described before, isn't it?" she asked him.

He nodded but remained quiet.

"What?" Janet looked up, but her confused expression let Cheryl know that she couldn't see anything at all. "What is it?"

Neither of them answered her.

Cheryl turned back around, and the tall thin ghost had vanished. Frank's eyes snapped open. He reached his hands up and grabbed hold of the railings on his hospital bed, knocking Cheryl's hand away. Then he opened his mouth, and sound poured out. It started as a long, low other-worldly rumble that vibrated the wall of Cheryl's chest. The pitch slowly rose until he was letting out a blood-curdling scream.

Janet covered her ears with her hands. "Stop it!" she yelled.

As if obeying her command, he stopped. He closed his mouth and his eyes. Letting go of the railings of the bed, he placed his hands on his stomach. His whole body relaxed almost as if he was melting into the mattress, and his breath returned to the deep breathing of sleep. Everything in the room had gone back to the way it was before. It would've been easy for Cheryl to think none of what she saw had happened at all, but that wasn't the case.

Janet let out a heavy sob. She pulled the tissue from her pocket and wiped her eyes. "I can't take this anymore." She turned and, shoving past Adam, fled the room.

Cheryl turned to Adam with her arms folded across her chest. "Is that what you saw earlier?"

"Pretty much." He stepped into the room for the first time since they had arrived.

"Did you see the man standing on the other side of the bed?"

He looked across the room as if hoping he would see the man now. "No."

"He was there. He's her ghost."

Adam came closer to her. "What did he say?"

"Nothing yet." Cheryl looked behind her, where Frank still lay sleeping in his bed as if nothing had happened. "But I'll make him talk." She laughed, realizing how gangster she sounded.

Janet appeared in the doorway, holding a crumpled tissue in her hand.

"We're going to fix this." Adam reassured her. "It will be scary, but we've done this before. Cheryl knows what she's doing."

Cheryl watched him. He was so sure about what she could do. She wished she had the same confidence in herself.

"You saw something just then in the room with him, didn't you?" Janet asked.

Cheryl nodded. "There was a man standing across the bed from me." Cheryl described him to Janet, who looked at her in wide-eyed disbelief.

"That's the ghost? That's the one causing all these problems?" Janet pulled nervously at the hem of her sweater.

Cheryl cleared her throat. "I don't know. He could be." She hadn't told Janet about the swirling hole in the ceiling and the frightful creatures dancing around inside it. She was more confident they were causing the problems than the giant ghost she saw.

Janet came into the room. She stood at her husband's bedside, gazing down at him. "When Frank got sick, I thought that would be the worst of it. I'm still coming to terms with the idea of him not being here with me one day, but now there's all of this too." She wiped her eye with a tissue.

It pained Cheryl, seeing someone suffer like this. "Like Adam said, we're going to do everything we can to help you."

Janet turned around to face them. "I would give anything if you could make Frank's last days on this earth peaceful."

"We'll do our best." Adam looked around the room. "I should check the cameras. Then I'm going to move one into here."

A worried look crossed Janet's face.

"Unless you don't want me to," Adam said.

"I just don't want the nurses to think I'm spying on them. I haven't told any of them about what's going on."

"Yvette already saw what's going on today. Do you want to talk to the others?" Adam asked.

"Yeah. Let me do that."

They all nodded in agreement.

Adam went upstairs to look at the cameras he had put there, leaving Janet and Cheryl alone to talk. They left Frank in the room to sleep and went into the living room, where they sat on the shabby floral couch. "Tell me about your husband. Maybe if I find out some more details about him, I'll be able to figure out why this is happening."

Janet shifted uncomfortably in her seat. "What's Frank have to do with any of this? Shouldn't you be finding out about the house?"

Cheryl angled herself toward Janet. "There are many factors that play key roles in hauntings. It's important that we check every possibility. Sometimes a house holds a dark energy that attaches itself to the occupants. Sometimes the ghost isn't attached to a place at all. It's seeking out a specific person to right a wrong, whether real or perceived. In either case, the truth of the matter is that once a ghost attaches itself to a specific person, whether because of where that person lives or they are seeking revenge, they remain attached to that person no matter where they live. People often mistakenly think that houses are haunted, but in reality, once you are able to perceive the spirits around you, it's you who are haunted. You and Frank could move, and whatever this is would still haunt you."

"But why would it be happening now?" A tear slid down Janet's cheek.

"Spirits need to find a weak point in order to wedge

themselves into your life. Frank is sick, and you are in a vulnerable emotional state."

Janet sniffled. "Sorry."

"Don't apologize. Your reactions to what's happening are natural, but that's why these ghosts are here now. They wait for the energy in the home to be just right, and then they attack." Cheryl watched Janet, trying to read her reactions to what she was saying.

Janet slumped her shoulders. "That's not reassuring."

"It should be." Cheryl had learned to be a lot more optimistic about the situations. "All we have to do is find out what the ghost wants and resolve it. Then all of this will go away." She waved her hand in the air like she was demonstrating a magic trick. "You don't have to sell your house and run away. We'll work together to resolve the problem, and then everything will go back to normal."

Janet raised an eyebrow at her. "And you can do that?"

Cheryl smiled. "Well, that's why you hired us, isn't it?"

Adam bounded down the stairs with the camera in his hand.

"Did you find anything?" Cheryl asked him, excited to know what was on the video.

Adam surprised her when he shook his head. "Nothing here. And your bathroom is back to normal too."

"That's surprising. It's almost never normal these days," Janet said. "So not seeing anything on the video is good, right?"

"It's not good or bad. It's just the way it is. Sometimes cameras get something. Sometimes they don't. No matter what, we are still going to try to figure out what happened. Sometimes cameras aren't the best tool to use," he said.

"What was Frank like? How did you two meet?" Cheryl thought if she did a bit more digging she'd learn something useful.

"You make me feel like he's already dead." Her voice had a soft breathy quality.

"I'm sorry. I don't mean to..." She stumbled over her words.

"That's okay." Janet reached out and touched her upper arm. "I know what you mean." She looked at her lap for a moment as if trying to figure out what to say next. Then she began.

Chapter 12

Janet got a sparkle in her eye. "Frank is funny and vibrant and always willing to try something new. That's why I fell in love with him. He helped me step out of my comfort zone and look at life in a whole new way. Five years ago, we went skydiving." She chuckled. "Can you believe that? Me... skydiving?" She shook her head, and a smile spread across her face. "He could talk me into anything."

"You're braver than me," Cheryl said.

"Not really. I was terrified, but Frank..." She looked at a spot across the room. Then she eased herself up off the sofa and walked over to the bookshelf on the other side of the room. Picking up a picture of her and Frank together, she said, "We went to the Grand Canyon last year. I'd never been before. Have you?"

Cheryl shook her head.

Janet walked over to Cheryl, who had remained on the sofa, and handed her the picture. In it, Janet and Frank stood with their cheeks pressed together, filling much of the frame. Only a sliver of the brick-colored cavern of the Grand Canyon was visible behind them. She thought it was funny that of all the pictures they'd probably taken of their trip, this was the one they chose to display.

"It must've been a fun trip." Cheryl looked at the photo for a few moments before returning her gaze to Janet.

Janet settled on the sofa next to her again. "It was amazing. Better than skydiving because I didn't feel like I was going to die." She let out a stifled laugh.

Cheryl laid the photo on the sofa between them.

"Frank is a thinker. He likes to solve problems, whether it be a puzzle or crossword or figuring out why the car is making that weird sound. When we were in Arizona, we happened upon the oddest little antique shop. It had a lot of interesting things. Frank found this ancient-looking book of riddles and couldn't resist buying it. We brought it home, and he forgot about it.

"Anyway, he started getting sick, and we found out it was"—she blinked back tears—"cancer. When we first got his diagnosis, it became another problem for him to solve. He doesn't give up easily. He read everything he possibly could about treatments. Sometimes he felt like he knew more than the doctors. Because of that, he also knew when the treatments weren't working. He was ready for all of this long before I was." She held out both her hands and gestured around the room. "I don't think I ever could've been—" Her voice hitched.

Cheryl reached out and put her hand on Janet's shoulder.

Janet straightened up and dabbed her eyes with the tissue. She pulled her shoulders back, trying desperately to compose herself. "I'm sorry, you're asking about the haunting, and I'm rambling on."

"I'm asking about anything you're willing to tell me. There could be a clue about what's going on in the most unlikely of places." The ceiling creaked overhead as Adam walked around the second floor. "Why did you tell me about the book he bought in Arizona?"

"Oh, right. Thanks for putting me back on track." She dabbed her eyes with the balled-up tissue. "He was spending a lot of time in the hospital getting his chemotherapy and tearing through those little Sudoku books. Then he remembered the antique riddle book he'd bought and started taking that to the hospital with him. This might sound crazy, but something wasn't right with that book."

"Like what?"

She thought for a moment. "Every time I saw him with it, I felt—" She bit her lip. "—I felt a bit sick inside. I even asked him to get rid of it. He laughed and said I was being ridiculous." Janet got up and wandered back over to the bookshelf on the other side of the room. "It must be here somewhere." She ran her fingers along the multicolored book spines on the shelf. "I never liked the look of the thing, but Frank was into it—the novelty of it." She put her hands on her hips and stood looking at the shelf. "It's not here."

"What's it called?" Cheryl got up from the sofa and stood next to her in front of the bookshelf.

"I don't know. I never noticed the title. It might not have had one." Janet put her finger to her chin and thought for a moment. "Where could it be?" She turned around and marched through the living room and into the hallway. Cheryl followed her.

With a determined stride, Janet walked up the stairs. "It might be in there." She pointed at the shut bathroom door.

"It's okay in there. No sludge, I checked." Adam, who had been looking at the camera in the upstairs hallway, brushed past her as he pushed the door open.

Janet gasped, covering her mouth with her hand.

With a sweeping gesture he motioned to the now clean

white space. "It's all normal now."

It wasn't normal though. Cheryl could feel that as soon as she stepped inside. Darkness pressed into her. She placed her hand on the wall to steady herself.

Janet stood in the doorway with a look of shock on her face. "I don't understand." She stepped inside onto the shiny white tile like she thought the floor would open up and swallow her. "There's been all that black goo coming out of the toilet, sink, and in the bathtub. No one else could see it but me until Adam came over earlier. And now it's gone." She met eyes with Adam.

Cheryl leaned against the wall and tried to take a deep breath, but she felt like a weight was pressing on her lungs. The music started playing in her head, a gentle thumping. "Not now," she said firmly.

Adam and Janet looked at her.

She shook her head. "It's nothing, just another ghost who wants my attention."

"The ghost that's here?" Janet asked.

"No. Unfortunately this is a completely different ghost."

"Do they try to talk to you often?" Janet looked at her curiously.

Cheryl snorted. "All the time."

The tall thin ghost she'd seen standing over Frank's bed appeared in the corner.

"We're not alone." She nodded toward him.

"There's a ghost in here now?" Janet looked around with wide eyes.

"He's in the corner over there. Is that where the book is?"

Janet nodded. "It should be. Can I get it? Is it safe?"

"Yes." Cheryl was sure about that. This ghost didn't seem to be the source of everything going on in the house.

Janet tiptoed into the bathroom and squatted in front of

a large wicker basket that sat on the floor across from the toilet with books and magazines piled high inside. Books clunked together as she rifled through them carelessly. Finally, she held up a small navy-blue hardcover book. "This is it." She whirled around on the balls of her feet and extended the book toward Cheryl.

As soon as she picked the book up the ghost disappeared. "He's gone." She hoped that would make Janet feel more at ease.

Janet held her hand to her heart. "Thank, God." She held the book out in front of her.

Cheryl took it. When she turned to leave the room, she got a glimpse of the mirror above the sink and she saw herself crying. Tears slid down her face and her mouth was opened in a pained scream. She froze and looked at the image of herself. It was like she was watching a video played on a loop, not her own reflection.

"Can you see that?" She pointed at the mirror.

"What?" Adam asked.

When Janet and Adam looked at the mirror, the image vanished, replaced with her reflection.

"That thing is evil." Janet picked up the rumpled sheet draped over the sink faucets and threw it over the mirror, covering it completely. "Nothing good happens when you look in there."

"What did you see?" Adam looked at the sheet that now hung over it.

"I thought I saw myself crying." She blinked a few times as if doing so would change something. "Anyway, let's take a look at this book." She went out into the hallway. She needed to get out of that bathroom. Janet and Adam followed her. The smooth hardbound book had no title on its worn cover. She looked at the spine, and there was no writing there either.

"It's a weird little book, isn't it?" Janet said.

Cheryl opened the book. The first page was blank, as was the second. On the third page, in Gothic-style text that seemed too on-the-nose to be real, it read, "Let's see how clever thou be, solve these riddles, then count to three."

"Corny." Adam snorted as he read over Cheryl's shoulder. "This has to be some kind of joke. There's no way it's real."

Disappointment shrouded Janet's face. "Okay. Maybe not. I was hoping it would give us the answer to something. Frank whispered the word 'book' to me earlier. At first I had no idea what he was talking about, but the more I thought about it, the more I started to think he must be talking about this." She puckered her lips and drew her eyebrows down. "Now that you're looking at it, I'm not so sure. There's no way this has anything to do with the haunting, right? I mean it's just a silly book of riddles."

Cheryl turned the next page to reveal a bunch of words scattered randomly with big spaces between them. Adam read them aloud. "Smoke, Odyssey, Incantation, Death, Life, Renewal." He chuckled. "What is it, some kind of strange word association game?"

She flipped another page to reveal more text written on a spiraling circle around the page. "This is crazy." Cheryl tilted her head as she read the words, which she couldn't make sense of at all. "What language do you think this is?"

"I don't know," Janet said. "That's one of the reasons Frank got the book. He loves languages. He speaks five."

Both Adam and Cheryl looked at her. "That's amazing," Adam said. "I can barely speak one."

Cheryl turned another page to reveal a solid block of text form a perfect square. The letters all butted up against each other with no spaces between them. "It's like one of those find the word games." She squinted at the letters that were so small they seemed to run together the longer she looked at them. She flipped to the book's center where the writing wasn't in roman letters anymore but an organized sequence of squiggles and dots. "Is this Arabic or something?"

Adam's grip tightened on her shoulder. "Do you see that?"

Cheryl glanced at his shocked face before turning her attention back to the book. "What?"

"What is it?" Janet parroted.

Adam reached over and snatched the book from her.

"Hey!" Cheryl spun around to look at him.

He stared at the page. "The words... They're jumping off the page at me."

**

Lines of text danced off the page forming shapes in the air that seemed to call out to Adam. In his excitement, he snatched the book from Cheryl. Its yellowing pages warmed his hands.

Cheryl and Janet stared at him, their mouths agape. "It's the book." His words bounced from his tongue. "It definitely has to do with the book."

"Seriously? We have to get rid of it, then." Janet reached her hand out to take the book away from him. "We should burn it."

The idea of burning such a magical relic seemed blasphemous to him. He recoiled at the mere sound of the word. He pulled the book into his chest, keeping it out of reach. "No!"

Janet looked at Cheryl, who raised her eyebrows. "What was that about?" she asked him. She turned to Janet before he could answer. "Getting rid of the book won't necessarily stop whatever has been going on here, but the book probably has clues that will help us."

"She's right. B-b-burning the book is no guarantee of a solution." Why did he stumble over the word like that? "We have to understand what it is so we can understand what it has done to Frank and your house." He lowered the book from his chest and looked down at it again. The words continued to glow and dance. "I know just the person to show it to. He'll know exactly what it is."

"The shopkeeper?" Cheryl asked.

Adam gave a firm nod, too enthralled by the book to answer aloud.

"Adam's right. Getting rid of whatever is haunting your home is not as simple as destroying this book. Frank might've unleashed something in your house, and we have to find a way to undo whatever he's done. Otherwise, it will keep happening." Cheryl spoke in a calm, measured tone.

There was nothing measured about the way Adam felt. He wanted to take the book, then run from the house and hide it away so only he could look at it. He was privileged that it was showing him its secrets. Now he had to figure out how to decode them. He looked down at the book again. The markings still glowed and seemed to hover just above the paper. Cheryl talked to Janet, but he didn't pay attention to what she said because he was too enthralled. He was so engrossed that he jumped when he felt a hand on his arm. He looked over to see Cheryl and Janet looking at him expectantly.

"Right, Adam?" Cheryl said.

He had no idea what they had been talking about but knew from experience that it was probably just best to agree. He nodded. When they continued to look at him, he realized he needed to say something more. "What Cheryl said is exactly right." His gaze drifted back to the twisting shapes hanging in the air in front of him.

"Are you sure this person will know what the book is?" Janet asked, bringing him back to the present moment.

"Ah, yeah. He'll definitely know something." His words trailed off as he returned his attention to the book. Cheryl grabbed hold of his arm, pulling him out of the room. Reluctantly he shut the book and walked with them down the stairs.

"Was there anything else on the cameras?" Janet asked as they went.

"No, but that doesn't mean they won't pick up something later, so I left them set up." Eagerly he gripped the book in his hand, feeling the weight of it. It was as if it were a living thing, and he couldn't wait to be alone with it.

They walked together toward the front door.

"Call us if anything serious happens." Cheryl was still talking to Janet in hushed tones as Adam hurried out the door to the car. The book seemed to vibrate in his hands. The car chirped as he unlocked it. He climbed inside, opening the book in his lap again before Cheryl even made her way to the car. When he looked up through the windshield, she was still standing on the porch talking to Janet.

The book fell open naturally to a page in the middle. Markings rose into the air in a swirling spiral. The wind from it lifted his hair. The moment entranced him. As he watched the hypnotic forms twisting before him, the world around him seemed to drop away. It was almost as if he was floating in space. Then the car door slammed, jolting him back.

He turned to see Cheryl looking at him with deep creases between her eyebrows. "Are you okay?"

He looked back down the book, and it appeared to be a normal book, just markings on the page in a language he didn't understand. "Yeah." He wanted to say more, but something inside compelled him not to.

"Can you take that to the shopkeeper tonight?" She nodded toward the book.

"If I can find the store." He hoped he could conjure it into existence whenever he needed it. That is what the shopkeeper had implied last time he saw him.

"Can I come too?" She reached over and took the book from his lap.

He fought the urge to slap her hand away. Instead, he let her take it. The muscles in his shoulders tensed as he watched her flip through the pages. "Maybe I should go by myself."

She sighed. "You probably should. I have to make sure I'm home in time for my next phone shift."

"You've been doing so many of those recently." He looked at the book as he talked to her.

"A girl's gotta do what a girl's gotta do." She flipped the page and held the book close to her face examining the text. "I wonder what language this is?"

"I don't know, but whatever it is, that's no ordinary book." He stared at the book now in her lap.

"Hopefully it will have the answers we need to get whatever presence is in that house out." Cheryl leaned her head back in the seat and closed her eyes for a moment.

He stopped at a red light and reached over, taking the book from her lap. Just holding it in his hands made him feel good. "I can't explain it. Ever since I touched this book, I feel like I have to be touching it to feel okay."

"I don't like the sound of that." Cheryl frowned at him.

The light turned green, but Adam didn't notice because he was looking down at the book in his lap. The car behind him honked, and he put his foot on the accelerator, taking off a little too quickly. The tires squealed. "It's fine. I'll find the shopkeeper and see if he knows anything."

"Yeah, but if it's affecting you strangely, I don't want anything to happen—"

"Nothing's going to happen." He raised his voice as he cut her off.

She drew her eyebrows together, opening her mouth to speak, then shutting it again as if thinking better of it. She shifted in her seat, turning her back to him to gaze out the window.

They didn't talk on the rest of the drive back to her place. Adam didn't want to talk. He wanted to get all this driving over with so he could look at the book again. What would it show him?

Chapter 13

Adam's behavior left Cheryl feeling uneasy. As she climbed out of the car, a feeling of dread settled in her chest. "I don't feel good about this." She nodded toward the book.

"I'll be fine."

She cocked her head at him. "I'm not so sure about that."

"It's fine. You have to get to work."

She did have to go, so reluctantly she got out of the car. As she walked up the stairs to her apartment, her head filled with that familiar disco beat again. It overran her thoughts, making it impossible for her to worry about anything else. "I don't have time for this right now," she muttered to herself as the volume of the music increased.

She pushed the door to her apartment open to reveal the disco. She jutted out a hip and sucked her teeth. Then she looked behind her to see if anyone else was in the hallway. Briefly, she considered turning around, walking down the steps, and back out onto the street.

"Enough! Enough! I can't take any more of this blasted noise!" Mr. Duncan's voice reached her ears before she saw him. She turned to see him standing in front of his door.

She looked over at him, standing there in a pair of creased khaki pants and a button-down shirt far too large for his slight frame. He held his hands in tight fists at his sides. His white mustache was like a broom resting above his lip. His thin gray hair stuck out in wisps atop his head. His usually pinkish complexion was now sallow.

"You look terrible." Cheryl spoke without thinking. Mr. Duncan was in his late seventies but always quite well put together. He would not normally step outside his apartment in such a state. "What happened?" Realizing the harshness of what she had said, Cheryl's hand flew up to cover her mouth as if she could stuff the words back inside herself.

He brought his hand up toward his face and waved a crooked finger at her. "What happened? Your constant partying happened! I can't get any sleep with all this racket. I can hardly hear myself think."

Suddenly, a light went on in Cheryl's head. "Wait a minute. You shouldn't be able to hear this music."

"Everyone in the whole building can hear it." He held out his arms in exasperation.

"No, they can't."

As if on cue, the sullen teenage girl who lived on the floor above them came down the stairs. Her long dark hair hung over her face, and she looked down at her phone as she walked. Her combat boots, which were inappropriate for the hot weather, clumped loudly on the stairs as she went. Cheryl couldn't remember her name. She didn't know if she'd ever been introduced to the girl even though she had spoken to her several times in the hall.

"Hey, excuse me." Cheryl waved her hand at the girl.

The girl looked up from her phone, startled that they would be speaking to her. She pointed at herself and cocked her head.

"Do you hear any music?" Cheryl asked the girl.

She squinted and looked from Cheryl to Mr. Duncan, the corners of her mouth drawn down disapprovingly. "No." Without hesitation, she returned her gaze to her phone and continued down the stairs.

"That's impossible. It's so loud." Mr. Duncan walked over to the staircase, gesticulating with his arms. "Don't tell me you can't hear that."

The girl was walking down the stairs away from him now. She didn't bother to look back at them but shook her head as she went, continuing to look down at her phone.

"I swear the young people are deaf these days. They run around with those things in their ears all the time." He pointed a trembling finger at his ear.

"I heard that," the girl, now out of sight, yelled at them up the stairs.

Cheryl chuckled. "She doesn't seem deaf to me."

Mr. Duncan let out a puff of air and crossed his arms over his chest.

Cheryl looked into her apartment, where the dancing scene continued. The music pumped and throbbed. If Mr. Duncan could hear the music, did that mean he could see what she saw too? "Come over here for a minute. I want you to see something." She motioned for him to come to her.

He scowled. He seemed to be getting grumpier by the minute. "Whatever you're trying to show me, I'm sure I don't want to see it."

Undeterred, Cheryl walked over and took him by the crook of his bony arm. "Come on. Just look. The sooner you do, the sooner I can make this music stop." She walked with him to her doorway. "What do you see in my apartment?" She stopped with him right at the doorway and motioned for him to look inside. Colorful lights flashed, and people danced enthusiastically to the disco beat. Cheryl saw the crowd, the shiny floor, the flashing lights.

Mr. Duncan looked through the open door blankly. "What am I supposed to be seeing exactly?"

Cheryl looked at his profile. His head craned forward, giving him the appearance of being in danger of tipping over. "You don't see anything unusual?"

"I see a cat. Is that unusual?"

Beau had come to the door. Sitting directly in front of them, he flicked his tail back and forth.

Cheryl bent down and picked him up. "But you still hear music, right?"

Mr. Duncan gave a firm nod. "The music never stops these days. I don't know how you do it." He sounded more in awe than angry this time.

"Interesting." Cheryl stepped inside her apartment. The dancers bopped and gyrated around her. Even though she was in danger of dropping into another time, she did her best to focus on Mr. Duncan to keep her in the here and now. She could feel Beau's body vibrate as he purred in her arms. "I promise you the music isn't coming from me. You can come into my apartment and check if you like."

Reluctantly he stepped over the threshold into her apartment, and as soon as he did, the music stopped, and the dancers vanished. "Well." He threw his arms up in the air. "It's quiet now. You probably turned it off with a remote control or something." He had only gotten two steps into the apartment when the ghost in black appeared, standing directly behind him. He stared at Mr. Duncan with sad brown eyes.

"Mr. Duncan, do you know anything about what this place used to be before it was an apartment building?" Cheryl could have kicked herself for not realizing it from the beginning. If Mr. Duncan could hear the music too, then of course the music and this ghost were all meant to send some kind of message to him. Why hadn't she thought of it earlier?

His dog barked from inside his apartment. "I haven't got time for this nonsense." He turned around and marched out the door. "Daisy is lonely."

"You lived here in the seventies, didn't you?" she called at his back as he continued to walk away. "I hear it was a lot different here back then."

He didn't answer. He just kept walking away from her.

With Beau still in her arms, she followed him. "Rumor has it this place used to be a dance club, but there was some kind of incident here. A lot of people died. Do you know anything about that?"

His steps faltered, and she thought he would turn around and answer her, but he didn't. He regained his stride.

"Did you know a black man with an Afro? He was tall and broad with a gap in his front teeth."

His step faltered again before he picked up his pace. Now it was almost as if he was running from her. He grabbed hold of his doorknob.

"Do you know him? I feel like you do. What if I told you he had a message for you?" Cheryl wasn't usually this aggressive about the messages she got from ghosts, especially when she didn't have a clear message yet, but the loud music had been driving her insane too. Like Mr. Duncan, she just wanted it to stop.

"I don't know what kind of game you're playing, but it's not funny." He spat the words at her before going into his apartment and slamming the door.

Cheryl ran up to his door and knocked. "Mr. Duncan, I could tell by the way you reacted that you know something. I'd love to talk to you about it. I think I know—" She didn't continue because she realized she didn't know anything.

Around every corner, there were questions, but she hadn't found any solid answers yet. She knocked on his door again, thump, thump, thump. This time she said nothing at all. She heard the click-clack of his dog's nails on the floor but nothing else inside his apartment. She could imagine him standing at the other side of the door perfectly still, waiting for her to go away. "When you're ready to talk, I'm just next door." She waited for a few moments before returning to her apartment. Her living room was thankfully empty. The ghost in black was gone for now, but she knew that wouldn't last long.

**

The book was trying to tell him something. Adam sat in his car with the dome light on in front of Cheryl's apartment building with the book open in front of him, trying to make sense of what he was seeing.

He studied the unfamiliar markings on the page. The lines and dots felt important even though he didn't know their meaning yet. He would find out though. He was determined to find out.

A chorus of discordant voices drifted into his thoughts, repeating the same phrase over and over again. He focused on the words in a language he didn't understand—angry sounding guttural syllables. He moved his mouth, trying to form the words along with the chorus of voices. Before he could figure out the long phrase, someone knocked on his window, startling him. The voices stopped. Adam glanced out his car window. A rail-thin man with a pale complexion looked in at him. It was already dark, and the light from the streetlamp cast dark shadows across the stranger's face. The man leaned closer to the glass and smiled, revealing a row of chipped, brown teeth.

Adam put his car into reverse and backed out of the parking spot. He didn't know what the man wanted, and he didn't want to know. He was about to head back home when he remembered he needed to find the shopkeeper. So, he went to Central Avenue and found a place to park. It was a balmy evening. Couples ate outside in front of restaurants, and people milled about on the streets in groups. He got out of the car with the book and walked in no particular direction up Central Avenue. He remembered what the shopkeeper had told him before. If he needed to find the shop, he would be able to, and he needed to find the shop right now. He concentrated on what the shop looked like in his mind, the green door, the swirly letters of the writing overhead. He had walked nearly two blocks when he finally saw it. The bright green door beckoned him. He ducked inside without hesitation, and the shop bell chimed, announcing his entrance. The store was empty, just as it usually was when he went inside.

Though the magic of the place still made him feel uncomfortable, there was something about the soothing music and the crowded bookshelves that calmed his nerves. He walked to the center of the store, where trays of crystals and stones lay on display. He picked up a smooth flat piece of cat's-eye and ran his thumb along the cold surface. The shopkeeper opened the door behind the counter and stepped out into the shop. "What do you have there?" He looked at the book in Adam's hand and raised his brow.

Adam returned the cat's-eye to its tray. Then he held the book up so the shopkeeper could see the cover, blank and faded. "I don't know. I was hoping you could help me with that."

Adam expected the shopkeeper to come closer, wanting

to examine the book, but instead of being excited about the mysterious book, he seemed to have trepidations. The shopkeeper remained glued to his spot behind the counter, unmoving. He wore a stern expression. "Where did you get it?" He continued to stare at the book in Adam's hand, never once letting it leave his sight.

"A client found it in a bookstore in Arizona." The book seemed to breathe beneath the grip of his fingertips. He felt a slow, steady expanding and contracting.

The shopkeeper frowned. "Why did you bring it here?"

"I was hoping you could take a look at it and tell me what it is." Adam walked forward with the book extended out in front of him.

The shopkeeper took several steps back. "Don't bring it near me." He held out his hand, telling him to stop.

Adam stopped abruptly, the rubber soles of his shoes squeaking on the tile floor. "Why not? How are you going to tell me what it is if I can't bring it near you?"

"You have no idea what you've gotten yourself into."

"Apparently not." Adam's gaze shifted around the room. "Why don't you tell me?"

"Do you really want to know?" His eyes met Adam's.

"Of course I want to know. That's why I came here." Adam walked forward with the book and set it on the counter in front of the shopkeeper, who looked down at it with suspicion.

"There is a long history of cursed books. Many of them are handwritten grimoires that are nearly impossible to get hold of. They are locked away in collectors' safes. Have you heard about the book that was written by the devil?" He paused as if waiting for an answer.

Adam shook his head. Before any of this began to happen to him, he would've said he didn't believe in the devil. Now he wasn't so sure.

"Whether these books were written by the devil or demons themselves or just by people influenced by them doesn't really matter. What matters is the content and the very real results human beings like yourselves suffer when they foolishly or perhaps unknowingly decide to mess around with such powerful dark magic. This book"—he nodded toward the book on the counter—"is more than just a book. I suggest you get rid of it as quickly as possible."

Adam reached down and felt the rough cover beneath his fingertips. The book surged with energy, so much energy. He flipped it open, and the shopkeeper jumped back like he expected something to come out of it.

"Shut it," he snapped.

Adam obeyed, closing the book. "I only want to show you what's inside so you can tell me how I can help my client. What do you mean when you say it's more than a book?"

"Think of it as a key." He pressed his lips together and held his finger to them, thinking for a moment. "That's not quite right. Think of it as a combination lock. But once you figure out the combination, what you unleash isn't good. There are no prizes on the other side. There's just murder and chaos."

Adam laid his hand on the front cover of the book. It was warm beneath the touch as if alive. "I don't understand how that's possible. It feels so good to me."

"That's because you've already touched it. It was designed that way to cast a spell on any man who possesses it. You want to solve the mystery inside, don't you?"

Adam didn't want to remove his hand from the book, but he did only to prove it didn't have control over him. "If someone's already solved the mystery and opened the lock, what happens?"

The shopkeeper crossed his arms over his chest and looked down at the floor. When he looked up again, there was fear in his eyes like nothing Adam had ever expected to see from him. "It depends on which riddles they solve, which incantations they repeated. There are degrees to opening the door. You can throw it wide open and let everything out or open it just a crack."

"But what are you opening the door to?"

"You're opening the door to the land of the damned that many religions call Hell. If you open that door wide enough, the devil himself could step through. If you open it just a crack, maybe you'll get a couple of damned souls or a few young demons. Everything happens in degrees. But a door that's open just a crack can eventually get pushed all the way open, and you don't want that to happen."

A chime sounded and the door to the shop swung open, startling Adam. He had assumed he was the only person who could see the shop. A young redhead walked in. She smiled at the shopkeeper, but confusion crossed her face for a brief moment when she saw Adam standing there.

Adam turned back to the shopkeeper. "If someone's already opened the door, how do I close it?"

"The same way you close any door." The shopkeeper turned his attention away from Adam to the girl standing by the door. "Ruth, come in. What can I do for you?"

"What does that mean?" he asked.

The shopkeeper frowned at him. "Do the exact opposite of what you did to open it?"

"How do I know what that is?"

The redhead watched Adam curiously but said nothing.

"I have another customer to take care of. You need to ask whoever opened it how they did that and then do the opposite." He glanced at the book. "Get that out of my sight."

Adam picked up the book from the counter and walked out of the shop, feeling a bit more confused than he had when he walked in.

Chapter 14

"I got some news for you," Stephanie said.

Cheryl sat on the floor between her sofa and her coffee table with the phone in front of her on speaker as she braided her mass of unruly curls. "Did you find something out about my ghost?"

"I sure did." The enthusiasm in Stephanie's voice made Cheryl happy. She had been going through so much recently. "I looked into your building first, and there used to be a dance club there called Dance! Dance! Dance! On June 2, 1976, seventy-eight people died there. They're still not exactly sure what happened. Some say it was some kind of chemical leak in the air-conditioning, probably Freon, but others say it killed people too quickly to have been Freon."

"Was it an accident?" Cheryl finished braiding her hair and pushed herself up onto the couch.

"That's what they think. I didn't see anything about suspicion of foul play."

"And it was this building?"

"Yes. The area where the disco was built in 1944, and they added your area where the apartments actually are in 1967." Stephanie spoke slowly, like she was referring to notes.

"What about the ghost? Did you find anything about him? A name maybe?" Cheryl asked.

"I haven't seen him, but from what you described, I think he might be Roy Silver. He died in the incident along with his business partner Maria Chen. Witnesses say Roy actually got out but went back in when he realized people were dying inside." Stephanie paused. "Did I do a good job?"

"You did an amazing job. I might have to get you to do my research for me all the time. I just haven't had the spare time to do it recently."

Stephanie's voice brightened. "I'd love to do that. It gave me something to think about other than Will and how I didn't see that he was such a monster. If you need me to look anything else up for you, just let me know. It was fun."

"I'll keep that in mind."

"I have to go. I need to get to work. I'll talk to you again later." A car door slammed in the background.

"Thanks again, Stephanie."

"No problem."

Cheryl hung up the phone with a sense of relief. When she looked up, Roy Silver was standing in front of her.

"Roy Silver," she said aloud, watching to see if he'd respond.

He blinked at her.

"I know your name, and I know who you want to talk to, but I still need you to tell me what you want to say." She took a deep breath and looked into Roy's large, dark eyes. She saw regret there.

Roy opened his mouth to speak.

***

Adam had just walked into the building when Ethan came

up to him. It was like he was waiting for him.

"Hey, buddy. How are you doing?" He slapped Adam on the back.

"Busy, but good." Adam had the ancient book of riddles in his messenger bag. He couldn't bear to be separated from it for even a moment. So, he'd taken to carrying it everywhere with him and flipping through it anytime he had a spare moment.

"I was wondering when you would have time to come over to my place and wave some sage around or whatever you guys do."

"I told you before we don't do that. I only want to work on legitimate cases." Adam hurried to the end of the long hallway, where he shared a windowless office with three other IT technicians.

"How many legitimate hauntings can there possibly be around here." He made air quotes with his fingers when he said "legitimate."

"More than you think." Adam didn't bother to look at him when he spoke.

Ethan matched his stride. "Come on, man. Give a guy a break. I live in a house full of women, and I swear every time I come home from work, they're all hysterical. I need all the drama to stop so we can go back to normal. You know I'll pay you."

"Whether or not you'll pay me isn't the issue." Adam's phone buzzed in his pocket. He took his phone out and looked at it. It was a text from his sister. "It's my sister. I really need to text her back, and then I have work to do." He hoped saying that would be enough to get Ethan to leave him alone.

"Okay, but I really need you to make an appointment with me. It's important. My sanity depends on it." Ethan walked a few steps backward up the hall and pointed at Adam as he spoke.

"I can't make any promises, but if a spot opens up, I'll go check it out." Adam figured he could go there alone one day. It would only take a few minutes to look around. That would get Ethan off his case. Since Cheryl only wanted to work on real hauntings, he'd go alone. There was no reason to waste her time too.

He went into his office, and as soon as he set his messenger bag down on the desk, Sofia popped her head in the door. "Oh good, my favorite IT guy is in today." She smiled brightly. "My computer keeps crashing, and I have no idea why."

"I guess you'll be my first job of the day." He put his messenger bag under his desk. He bent over for a moment, pausing with his hand on it, not quite sure what to do. He didn't want to leave the book alone in his office. The idea of being separated from it made him feel anxious, but he knew walking around carrying it probably wouldn't be such a good idea either.

"Are you okay?" Sofia's voice interrupted his thoughts.

"Yeah." He stood, deciding he had to leave the book there even though he didn't want to. He walked over to the door to follow Sofia up the hallway.

"Any time I try to open a file, the screen goes blue, and then the computer completely shuts down. I don't get it."

He followed her up the hallway, only half-listening to her because as soon as he stepped away from the book, chanting filled his head, pushing away his other thoughts. He had no idea what these ancient-sounding words meant, but he felt compelled to repeat them. He restrained himself because he knew that probably wasn't such a good idea.

"Hey, Adam. Are you even listening to me?" She'd stopped in front of her office door and was staring at him.

"I'm sorry. What was that?" He did his best to focus on what she was saying and block out the ancient language in his head.

"I was asking if you want to get lunch later or maybe drinks after work?" She pushed her office door open.

"Yeah, sure." He wasn't really thinking when he answered.

"Good. I have to be in a meeting in a few minutes, so I'll leave you to it." She motioned to her desk.

"I'll probably have it all taken care of before you get out."

She smiled at him before heading up the hall to the conference room. Adam watched her go. Then he went into her office, knowing that Sofia's crashing computer was probably the easiest problem he'd have to solve that day.

***

Janet sat at the kitchen table, leaning on her elbows with her chin in her hands. The microwave behind her beeped, letting her know the leftovers she decided to reheat for breakfast were ready, but she didn't move. She stayed perfectly still, staring at the camera Adam had set up in the kitchen and wondering what was on it.

She was tired, physically and mentally. When Frank started going downhill, she knew it would be difficult, but she never expected to be dealing with ghosts at the same time. She had hoped that since they'd taken that terrible book away, everything would get a little better, but the feeling in the house only continued to get worse. As soon as she stepped over the threshold, she felt a dark presence surround her. When she and Frank bought this home, it had been everything they dreamed of, but now she couldn't stand being here. She had to be here though because this was where Frank was, and she had no idea how much time she had left with him.

The microwave beeped again. Then she heard something else, a man's voice whispering in her ear. "It's still here," the voice croaked.

Janet stood so quickly her chair fell, clattering to the floor behind her.

"Is everything okay?" Yvette called from the next room.

Janet took a few wheezing breaths, trying desperately to choke back a sob. "Everything's fine. I just knocked something over." She righted her chair. The refrigerator clicked on, the motor humming behind her as she tried her best to slow her breathing. Convincing herself she'd heard nothing, she went to the microwave and got her food out and put her plate of leftover lasagna on the kitchen table. It was a heavy breakfast, but did that even matter anymore? Did anything matter?

She sat down in the wooden chair at the table, and as soon as her bottom hit the seat, everything around her went red. It was almost like she had flipped the light switch. Red light washed over the whole kitchen. Janet gripped the table and screamed. At least she tried to, but when she opened her mouth, nothing came out. The world felt like it was rocking, and she had dropped into a fever-filled nightmare. The cabinet doors flapped back and forth like wings around her. She watched them in wide-mouthed terror. She looked down at her plate of food to see blood-red worms slithering out from between the noodles with ropes of cheese still stuck to their bodies. Their arrow-shaped heads pointed in her direction as they slithered over the plate. She jumped to her feet, but she was standing in something slick. Her feet almost slipped out from under her. She grabbed the table to keep herself from falling, squishing worms beneath her fingers. A man, so thin he could have been mistaken for a skeleton, stepped through the kitchen door. His sunken eyes stared at her from his emaciated face. He was charred and cracked all over. His skin curled back in places, revealing the wet pink flesh underneath it. He wore a dark suit that was tattered along the edges of the sleeves and the hem of the jacket. The jacket hung off him like he was a hanger. Smudges of dirt marked the front. His pants were bunched at the waist and held up by a fraying rope. He was small, about Janet's height, and when he walked, it seemed like he was slightly out of sync with the rest of the world. As he moved toward her, he stumbled, his knees buckling for a moment before catching himself. When he stood again, he twisted his neck this way and that, and his vertebrae let out loud crunching popping sounds.

When Janet took her hands from the table, she didn't even notice the slime from crushed worms covering her fingers. She stood upright on the slick floor, concentrating on not falling. She spun around and ran. Her feet slipping and sliding on the floor, she could barely keep herself upright as she made her way to the back door. When she got to where the back door should've been, there was nothing there but a solid white wall. Janet struck the wall with her hand. She knew this wasn't right. This was where the door should be—looking to her left and to her right, everything else in the kitchen seemed normal except for being bathed in red. The door should've been right here. She had gone through it thousands of times. She walked out into the yard to tend the garden and sit on the back deck. There was a door here. She knew it. She turned around and pushed her body against the wall. Her eyes closed because she was certain she would feel the strange man's hands around her neck at any moment choking the life from her. But she felt nothing, nothing at all. When she opened her eyes, he was still standing in the doorway. Hadn't he been coming toward her? Wasn't that why she was running away?

She tried to yell again, forgetting that her voice was gone. Again, nothing came out. What was happening? She didn't know, but she felt for certain that she would die in this room. Part of her didn't even care because at least she wouldn't have to live her life without Frank.

The man began to walk toward her again. The slickness of whatever was on the floor didn't hinder his movement.

Janet wanted to give up, but she couldn't without first saying goodbye to Frank. She had nothing to lose now, so if he was going to walk toward her, she was going to walk toward him. There was no place else for her to go anyway. She inhaled deeply. A pungent, sharp scent filled her nostrils. She stepped away from the wall on tentative legs, wary of falling. Then she marched toward him, looking into his dark, sinister eyes. She was not going to be a victim anymore. She would fight and fight and fight even if that meant certain death. Before she got to the man, another man appeared between them. This man was so tall his head nearly touched the ceiling.

Janet stopped dead in her tracks. Her feet slipped, and she waved her arms in the air to stop herself from falling. The tall man reached out his hand. His arm seemed to span the length of the kitchen. He grabbed hold of her collar, holding her upright, his massive hand at her throat. Then he let her go as soon as she regained her balance. He didn't look at her once. Instead, he stared in the direction of the shorter man. Janet never saw his face, but she heard him. He opened his mouth, and a sound, so loud the whole room shook, poured out. The china broke in the cabinet. The windows shattered. The floor shook beneath her feet. His scream was eardrum-rupturing loud. Janet put both hands over her ears and squatted down on the floor, tucking her face into her knees. She swore her internal organs were vibrating. She opened her mouth and tried to scream too, but still no sound came out. Everything around her seemed like it would blow apart from the deep terrible noise.

A hand on her back startled her. "What's wrong? What's happening?" Yvette's voice drew her out of the alternate world she was in. Janet looked up to see the nurse standing there. Her friendly round face stared down at her. Janet looked around the kitchen, and it was normal. There was no red light or no worms. Her plate of lasagna sat with steam still rising from it, waiting to be eaten.

"Are you okay? I heard you screaming." Yvette reached out her hand, and Janet took it, letting her help her find her way to her feet and to the kitchen chair.

Janet settled on the hard chair, her head still aching and her thoughts spinning. "You didn't hear that noise?" She still remembered how encompassing the large man's scream was.

"I only heard you screaming."

"What's happening? Is everything okay?" Frank's voice was weak and barely reached their ears in the kitchen.

"Yes," Janet called out, surprised that she could. "I thought I saw something." What did she think she saw? She couldn't even begin to explain. The last thing she wanted to do was worry Frank. She looked around the kitchen to find everything the way it should be. There were no broken dishes or shattered windowpanes.

"Are you sure you're okay?" Yvette had the kindest eyes. They searched her face now, looking for a clue about what had happened.

Janet gave a firm nod even though she wasn't very sure about anything. "I feel like I'm losing my mind. Maybe I should see a grief counselor or something."

"I think that's a good idea." Yvette twisted and looked back toward the hallway.

"What's going on?" Frank asked again, his voice even

weaker.

Janet sighed. There was no way she could explain to anyone what she had just seen and have them believe it. She didn't really believe it herself. Maybe she was right in thinking that all of this was just evidence of her not being able to deal with the sad reality that she was about to lose Frank. Was this what grief felt like to anyone else? "I should go tell Frank that I'm okay." She went to stand up, but she was so weak from everything that she couldn't quite bring herself to her feet.

"You don't have to right away." Yvette was still looking down at her with the most empathetic expression. "You can sit here and take a few deep breaths to get yourself together first. Maybe that would be better."

Janet waved her hand in the air dismissively. "I'm fine. I am together. Let me go talk to Frank. I don't want him to worry."

Frank's hospital bed was inclined, so he was sitting up. It was nice to see him awake because he was awake so little these days. Before he was sick, he was always so active; he always needed to have a busy mind. The skin around his jaw was tight and pulled into his face, giving him the same look the skeletal figure she'd seen in the kitchen had. Had she seen it? Everything in her life had become a question now.

"There you are. Are you okay? I heard you screaming," Frank's voice rasped. Since he had gone into palliative care, they had stopped chemo, and little tufts of hair grew on his head.

Janet inhaled deeply, promising to hold herself together. She walked into the room, placed her hand on his fuzzy head, and rubbed it playfully.

"I'm going to step outside for a minute," Yvette said. "Just come out and let me know when you're done."

"I'm glad you're awake. You've been so..." She started to

say that he'd been out of it but thought better of it.

"Zonked out." He smiled as he spoke.

"Exactly."

"Cancer will take it out of you."

Janet chuckled, but Frank's face grew grave. He looked toward the door before placing a bony hand on Janet's. "What happened in the kitchen?"

Janet shook her head. She never lied to Frank and didn't want to start now, but he was so sick. "Don't worry about it. I don't want to worry you."

He lowered his eyebrows, and his forehead creased. "You've seen them, haven't you?"

Janet widened her eyes. "Who?"

"They're always around. I see them all the time." He motioned with his head for Janet to lean in closer.

Tears pricked her eyes. "We need to get rid of them, but I don't know how. They're driving me crazy, Frank."

"That's what they're trying to do. They like it when you're off balance."

"How do we get rid of them?"

"I don't know."

"It's time for your medication." Yvette sauntered into the room.

Janet pursed her lips and nodded slowly. She didn't want to talk about this in front of her. "I should go eat breakfast. I left my food on the table. It's probably already cold." She leaned over and kissed Frank on the cheek.

"Be careful. They're everywhere," he whispered in her ear.

Chapter 15

Cheryl waited in hallway with Roy Silver standing next to her. She was grateful that he hadn't shown her the disco scene again. It was too early for dance music, and she desperately needed the brain space to think.

She hadn't seen Mr. Duncan since he fled into his apartment when she asked him about Roy Silver the day before. Now she had a distinct feeling he was avoiding her, but it was morning, and he would have to take Daisy out for a walk. He was far too neat and conscientious to let her relieve herself in his apartment. So, she decided to wait outside with Roy because, so far, talking to him had been fruitless, but that didn't mean she would stop trying.

"So, do you come here often?" she joked.

Roy didn't answer her. She hadn't expected him to. He hadn't answered a single question she'd asked him yet.

"Do you have a favorite dance?" She watched his face, trying to judge if he could even hear her. His expression was blank. "I can't remember a dance step to save my life. I'd rather make something up. Some people are line dance kind of people. I never really understood that. I'm not particularly interested in dancing in a group like that. If I'm going to dance, I need room to swing my arms and get into it. That only happens in my living room." She chuckled to herself, remembering how many times she'd danced around her living room to lift her mood. "Sometimes you need to dance the pain away, you know?" She pressed her lips together and pushed back that bruised feeling she sometimes got near her heart when she thought about the past. Sometimes she said too much. She hoped he couldn't hear her now. "How often do you dance around by yourself?" She smiled weakly. "You probably don't have time for that kind of foolishness." She sighed. She was tired of waiting, but Mr. Duncan wasn't giving her any other choice. He refused to answer his door when she knocked. "I'm sure you're an excellent dancer. Am I right? Do you ever do this dance?" Cheryl jabbed her finger in the air and rocked her hips back and forth. "It's a classic seventies dance move."

Roy finally looked at her, and a hint of a smile spread across his face. Encouraged, she spun around.

"What's going on out here?"

Cheryl looked up to see Mr. Duncan standing in his open doorway with Daisy at his side. He looked a bit more put together than he had the last time she saw him in a pair of Bermuda shorts that exposed his knobby knees and a polo shirt. His black socks were pulled up his calves, and he wore a pair of thick, white sneakers. With a look of disgust on his face, he attempted to maneuver past Cheryl, but Daisy dug in her paws and wouldn't move. The hair between her shoulders stood on end, and she began to bark. "Come on, girl." Mr. Duncan yanked at her leash, but Daisy wouldn't budge. Mr. Duncan shot Cheryl a wilting look.

Cheryl held up both hands. "I'm not doing anything. Why are you looking at me like that?"

He shook his head and yanked on Daisy's leash again.

"Since you're here, I was wondering if you could tell me about Roy Silver."

Mr. Duncan's whole body stiffened.

Cheryl looked at Roy, who shifted his gaze to watch Mr. Duncan.

Daisy's bark echoed through the hall.

"Come on, Daisy." Mr. Duncan pulled at the leash and tried to walk around Cheryl.

"You were at the club that night, weren't you?" She took a step toward him, and Roy did too. "I didn't realize, but you were the man with the mustache who stormed out of the club before everything happened." The pieces started to come together in her mind.

Mr. Duncan looked at her with wide eyes. Then he scowled and shook his head as if trying to shake something off. "You almost got me. I know what you do for a living. You research people and then you pretend you know something about their past. You're just a charlatan like the rest of them." Daisy growled at Roy.

"You can think what you like, but that doesn't change what's true. You should listen to me because I'm trying to give you good news." Cheryl wasn't sure if that last statement was true or not. She only hoped it was. She so much preferred giving good news, but didn't most people?

"You're telling me what I already know. That's not news." He tugged on Daisy's leash, trying to lead her around Cheryl, but Daisy resisted.

"On the night those people died in the club, you were here too." She tried her best not to make this sound like an accusation.

Tired of pulling on Daisy's leash, he threw out his arms. "So what if I was. It was decades ago."

"Because Roy has a message for you." She had to keep trying even though he clearly didn't believe her.

He blinked and his eyes grew glassy. "Roy's dead. He died with the rest of them right under where we're standing." He looked at the floor. "I..." His voice dropped off. "I have to go." He gave Daisy's leash another yank, but she still refused to move. "Come on, girl. Don't you want to go for your walk?"

A voice ricocheted around in Cheryl's head. She looked at Roy, whose mouth didn't move, but somehow, she knew the voice she heard was his. Without even thinking, she began to repeat the words aloud to Mr. Duncan. "Roy says that some of the happiest times in his life were spent with you. Remember when you drove down to Miami and the car overheated in alligator alley. That must've sucked," Cheryl interjected.

"It did," Mr. Duncan said.

"He says that one of his biggest regrets is that he wasted his whole life hiding from who he was."

Mr. Duncan looked at Cheryl. "How do you know that?"

"It's not me talking anymore. I'm telling you what Roy is telling me." Cheryl looked at Roy who stood directly in front of Mr. Duncan now. She could feel the regret seeping off him. "Charlie, I'm sorry. I should've told Maria sooner, but I was having a hard time accepting it myself. Funny thing is—" He let out a dry laugh. "—the funny thing is when I told her she said she already knew. She didn't even care. She acted like it was all a given. Then she told me that she had been seeing someone on the side for ages. She was just waiting for me to finally have the courage to tell her." He looked up. "Can you believe it?"

Mr. Duncan looked at Cheryl now with new eyes. She felt as if he was seeing something in her that he had never seen before. "When I heard about what happened, I couldn't believe it. I had just been there. It seemed so unreal. I hoped Roy had gotten out. I kept thinking that if I hadn't left early that night, I would've been able to save him." He stopped and his expression shifted. "I can't believe I'm falling for this carnival trick." His voice had a hard edge, but he didn't try to walk away this time. He stood glaring at her.

Cheryl didn't answer his question. Roy still had more to say. "I was outside when it started. I had no idea what was going on until people began pouring out of the club, covering their faces. I went back in because it was my club. I was responsible for everyone in there. I didn't expect to see so many people lying on the floor, dying. It was like a monster had come through. I found Maria first, and she was already gone by the time I got to her. I started to feel the chemicals taking the air out of me. Even with the rag over my face, I could tell that every breath I took contained less and less oxygen. I couldn't leave anyone in there to die though. I couldn't have lived with myself if there was something I could've done but didn't. It happened so quickly. All at once I fell over and I was struggling to breathe. Then it was like I went to sleep, but I never woke up. When I closed my eyes I saw you, Charlie. I saw your face looking at me, and I regretted every minute I spent hiding how I really felt. I just hoped you had gotten out."

"I did." He sniffled. "I guess I don't have to tell you that."

"I'm glad you did. I'm sorry I wasted so much time and we never got to see what could be."

"So am I." Mr. Duncan wiped a tear from his eye.

"Well," Roy put his hands in his pockets and stood casually, his shoulders slightly slumped. "I know why you stay here, but you don't have to be in this building to be close to me. I'll be wherever you go, looking out for you."

Mr. Duncan looked up at the ceiling inside. "I love you, Roy Silver. I miss you so much." Tears ran down his cheeks.

"I know, but you don't have to because I'll always be close by." Roy faded, leaving Cheryl and Mr. Duncan standing there alone.

"Was that real? It felt real." He took off his glasses and pulled a white handkerchief from his pocket. He blew his nose with a honk.

"Yes, it was as real as anything." The feeling of joy Cheryl had from sharing this moment was worth suffering through all the dance music that had been pounding in her head over the past few weeks. Ghosts often have difficulty communicating at first and would come up with their own unique ways to get their messages across. She'd hated dealing with Roy's unique method, but she was glad to have been a part of sharing this moment with Mr. Duncan. She reached out and gave his arm a reassuring squeeze. "You're lucky you got to hear that from Roy. Most people don't get that luxury after someone they love passes on."

"I know." He shoved his soiled handkerchief back into his pocket.

"So, you believe me now?"

He narrowed his eyes at her. "Part of me wants to believe."

"Listen to that part of you because I'm not trying to get anything from you. I'm just passing on a message from Roy." She understood. Not long ago she wouldn't have believed it either.

He nodded. "I never thought I'd be saying anything like this to you, but thank you. I always wondered what would've happened if things were different. I never knew how he really felt. If you're telling the truth, which despite myself I want to believe you are, I don't have to wonder anymore about how he felt at least." He looked down at Daisy who whined at him. "I need to get her out for a walk." He walked by Cheryl, and this time Daisy came with him easily. Before starting down the stairs he turned back to her. "You brought up a lot of memories." His eyes were glassy.

"I'm sorry."

"If you're being honest, you don't have to be sorry. I needed to know. I wanted desperately to know for decades." He went down the stairs.

As Cheryl went back into her apartment, she realized her mind was completely quiet. She wondered if the music would start up again during the day. She hoped it wouldn't because she knew that she needed every ounce of brain space she had to help Frank and Janet Tate.

Cheryl was eating breakfast when Adam knocked on her door. She'd been waiting for him. He kissed her roughly as he came in and handed her a cup of coffee.

"Since it's Saturday and we've been working really hard, I thought that after we check out what's on the cameras at the Tates from last night, we could go to the Saturday morning market or the museum or something." He looked at the pile of overdue bills on the dresser by her door. His expression changed.

She shook her head. "Don't."

"I hope none of these are utilities." He picked up a pink envelope and looked at it.

She shook her head. "They're all credit cards and hospital bills."

"Hospital bills?" He looked up at her.

She pointed to her belly where the scars from the night Mark attacked her lay hidden beneath her thin T-shirt, and he nodded knowingly. Sometimes she felt like she'd spend her whole life paying for her bad decisions.

"You know, my place has a view of the water. You could live there rent free and use the extra money to get all these bill collectors off your back."

The rent in her little apartment building was cheaper than in other places downtown, but it had gone up again this year. Freeing up that money to pay off her debts would help her get out of trouble so much faster. Even though Adam had never shown any indication that he was anything like Mark, the scar on her belly where the knife had gone in so many years ago was a constant reminder that she couldn't trust men too quickly. Mark had seemed fine too at first. She shrugged. "I've got it under control."

"It doesn't look like it to me." He put the envelope back down on the dresser.

He was right. She didn't, but admitting that would be too embarrassing. She took a sip of coffee. "Let's talk about something else. Did you see the shopkeeper yesterday?" She turned and walked into the apartment, returning to the table and her bowl of granola. "You want some?" She motioned to the bowl.

He shook his head. "I just shoved a croissant into my face."

"And you didn't get me one."

"It wasn't from the coffee shop. It was a stale one I had at home." He sat down at the table across from her. That was when she noticed that he had the book with him. He set it on the table.

She nodded toward it. "What did he say about it?"

"What did who say?"

"The shopkeeper, you saw him, didn't you?" She watched him. There was something unusual about him today that she couldn't quite put her finger on.

He looked down at the book before looking at her like he was trying to decide whether or not he would tell her something.

"What is it?" She poked at her granola with her spoon.

She could see the gears turning in his head like he was trying to decide what to say. She waited.

Finally, he spoke. "Yeah, I saw the shopkeeper." He paused.

"And...?" Cheryl leaned in.

He took a sip of his coffee, obviously stalling. "He said the book is dangerous. He wouldn't even touch it." Adam reached over and ran his hand along the cover. "That surprised me. It seemed like such an overreaction."

Cheryl's heart beat faster. "What do you mean dangerous?"

He took another sip of his coffee and looked down at the book. "He said a demon wrote it, and if you read certain passages out loud, the gates of Hell would open."

Cheryl sat back in her seat and crossed her arms over her chest. She eyed the book on the table.

"I don't know if I believe him."

Her gaze snapped back up to Adam. "Why wouldn't you believe him?"

He shrugged so casually it seemed strange. "It doesn't feel like anything dangerous. It feels important and life-changing."

She narrowed her eyes at him. "Maybe that's a trick to make you read from it." She reached across the table to grab the book, but Adam grabbed her arm. She flinched, throwing up her free arm to shield her face. Her heart raced.

He let go of her. "I'm sorry. I would never..."

She lowered her hand and pulled her arm across the table, lowering it into her lap. She could still feel the sensation of where he grabbed her a little too hard.

"If it's dangerous, maybe you shouldn't touch it." He placed his hand over the book protectively.

Usually, she wouldn't insist in a situation like this, but something was off. "I touched it before. I think I'll be fine." She tamped down the fear swirling inside her. She eased her hand back across the table and took the book. With it in front of her now, she flipped it open. "It worries me that you're so possessive of this."

"You don't have to be worried. It's fine." He stared at the book as she flipped through it.

"You said you saw words dancing off the page before. Have you seen those again since that first time?"

"Yes." There was a hesitation in his answer that she didn't like.

"Have you seen anything else strange related to the book?" She still looked down at the pages that were mostly jumbles of letters that made no sense at all to her.

"Nothing really." He hesitated again.

She looked up at him and saw the way he looked lazily off to the side as he talked. He always did that when he was hiding something. "How come I don't believe you?"

He shrugged. "I don't know. Why don't you believe me?" He looked at her, focusing on her eyes a bit longer than natural.

"Maybe because you're not telling me the truth. I'm like a lie detector, Adam. If there's been something strange going on, you have to tell me." In reality, she still didn't trust her judgment, but she'd spent so much time observing Adam, trying to decide if she could trust him that she'd become an expert at reading his cues.

Adam stared at the book in her hand like not having it was painful.

"If you tell me what's going on, I'll give you the book

back." She snapped it closed but continued to hold it firmly in both hands. "I can't make sense of it anyway."

"Honestly, neither can I." His gaze drifted up to her face. "I keep hearing these words in my head."

"What are they saying?"

"I'm not sure. They're in a different language, but they keep playing over and over again in my mind, making me want to repeat them. I have to fight hard not to." He took off his glasses and wiped the lenses on his T-shirt. "It's like I really want to say them, but I know I shouldn't."

Cheryl slid the book back across the table to him even though she didn't like the idea of him keeping it. "Maybe that's what happened with Frank. He repeated the word and opened the door."

Adam took the book from the table and held it in his lap. "That's what I think might have happened. That's the only reason I haven't said the words even though I really want to. I know there would be negative consequences." For the first time since he'd come into her apartment, she noticed his lips moving when he wasn't talking like he was mouthing words in rapid succession.

"What's that? What are you doing now?" She pointed an accusing finger at his mouth.

"What do you mean?" He looked back at her bewildered.

"You were just moving your mouth."

His lips were moving again, but he wasn't saying anything.

"You're doing it again." She jabbed a finger in the air at his face.

"I don't know what you mean. I'm not doing anything." He opened the book and flipped through the pages. The sense of relief on his face made Cheryl squirm with discomfort.

She got up from her chair and walked around the table.

Holding out her hand to him, she said, "Give it to me." She wiggled the fingers of her open hand.

He looked up at her in dismay. "What?"

"Give it back to me. I don't like the way you're acting. Maybe I should keep it for now."

He wrapped his fingers around the book, gripping it hard and looking up at her accusingly. "You don't know what to do with it. I have a connection with it, so I'm the person most likely to figure it out."

She reached down and tried to snatch the book from his grasp, but he was holding it too tightly. Cheryl wondered if she would have to fight him for it. She didn't want to, but what if she had to. They were in a tug-of-war over the book as she ran through the self-defense moves she knew in her head, trying to figure out what she could do to make him let go of the book without injuring him.

"I can't let you keep this. It's dangerous. You told me that yourself, and the way you're acting lets me know that it has a hold on you." Her voice strained as she talked. The book began to slide from her hands as he pulled it.

A telephone started ringing. She knew by the sharp old-fashioned ring that it wasn't hers. She raised an eyebrow at him, knowing that if he answered it, he'd have to let go of the book.

"You should get that. It could be an emergency." The slick words rolled off her tongue.

He scowled and let go of the book, causing her to fall back, but she caught herself before tumbling over the coffee table. The book flew from her hand and landed open on the floor.

By the time she regained her bearings, he was already talking on the phone. As he spoke, he casually got up from the table and strolled over to where the book lay. Anticipating his plan, she darted over to it and picked it up before he could. It was only after she had the book in her hands again that she paid attention to what he was saying on the phone.

"Okay. We'll be over right away." He hung up, and from the way he looked at her, she knew that something had happened at Janet and Frank's house. Their Saturday wasn't going to be relaxing after all.

Chapter 16

Janet was strangely calm when she opened the door. "Thank you so much for coming over on a Saturday. Come on in." She ushered them into the living room, where they stood uncomfortably. Adam immediately began looking around for something out of the ordinary. She'd sounded so panicked when she called, and now he couldn't see how this was an emergency at all.

"When I talked to you on the phone, you said something strange was happening?" Adam asked. He stuck his empty hands in his pockets and looked around the seemingly quiet living room. Cheryl had persuaded him to leave the book in the car even though he desperately wanted to carry it with him into the house.

"It happened in the kitchen. I'm hoping you caught something on camera." She motioned for them to follow her through the living room down the hall into the kitchen. They passed the bedroom where Frank lay sleeping. The same nurse, Yvette, who had been on duty before sat in the chair next to him, reading a book.

"How's your husband doing?" Cheryl asked.

Janet turned around, so she was walking backward for a few steps as she answered her. "Surprisingly well today. He almost seemed like his normal self this morning."

"That's good news." Cheryl smiled at Yvette as they walked by the doorway of Frank's room.

They stepped into the kitchen, where again everything seemed completely normal. Janet motioned with a grand gesture toward the table as she began her story. "I just heated up something for breakfast," she started and proceeded to tell the story about what had happened that morning.

As she talked, Adam went to the camera to see if he could find any evidence of the story she told on the video. Without the book, he needed to keep his hands busy to ease his anxiety.

Janet continued to talk quickly. Words whirled around so fast Adam could hardly keep up, but he didn't need to. He knew the story already because he had experienced similar things himself. He ran through the videos as she talked and immediately saw something. To many it might've looked like a glitch, but he knew his cameras, and they didn't glitch like this. A chunk of time was missing from one of the videos. The video showed Janet preparing breakfast. She took out what appeared to be leftovers from the refrigerator, put them on a plate, and stuck them in the microwave. Later she got it out and set it on the table, but as soon as she sat down the video went black and then stayed that way for maybe a second before coming to life again to show her on the floor with her hands over her ears yelling as Yvette walked in. Yvette placed her hand on Janet's back and said something. Then Janet sat in a chair while they talked. Then they left the kitchen together.

Cheryl sidled up next to him without him even noticing. "Anything?"

"There's a whole chunk missing from the video." He

played the video for her.

Janet came over to watch over their shoulder also. "Why did it stop recording there? Why would it stop when everything happened?"

"I'm not sure," Adam said.

"But you believe me, right?" she asked.

"We definitely believe you." She had no reason to lie. Adam had seen what was happening in the bathroom earlier and the vortex over Frank's bed. Then there was the mirror and everything with the book. There was no reason to doubt anything she said was true. "We just need to figure out what to..." The ancient chanting started again, rattling around in his brain and distracting his thoughts. The book wanted him to repeat it, but he knew he shouldn't. He'd left it in the car on the passenger's seat, hoping the distance would lessen the power it was gaining over him. Now he felt compelled to go to the car and retrieve it, but he wouldn't. The words tugged at his thoughts. They needed to be spoken. He moved his lips, silently forming the words.

"Are you okay?" Cheryl asked. She put her hand on his upper arm.

Adam tried to shake off the thoughts. "Yeah. I just got a bit distracted."

Cheryl narrowed her eyes at him before turning her attention to Janet. "Do you know if Frank solved any of the riddles in that book?"

"Or if he read any of the phrases from it aloud?" Adam was doing his best to resist doing that very thing, so it would make sense if that was the way Frank had accidentally opened the door to the other side.

Janet shook her head. "He said something about all of this being his fault, but I don't think he knows exactly how he did it, let alone how to fix it."

"If we could talk to him when he wakes up that would be helpful." Adam looked toward the kitchen doorway, where he could see a sliver of the bedroom where Frank slept.

"He's been asleep for a while. He might wake up before you go," Janet said.

"That would be good." Adam looked at Cheryl, but she wasn't paying attention to the conversation. She stared at the wall next to the kitchen door. Her face was frozen in fear.

**

Cheryl looked up and saw him walk through the wall. First a leg encased in dusty black pants appeared and then another. His right arm, then his left, his torso and his head eased through the wall like it was merely a curtain. Each body part appeared until he stood in front of her in the kitchen. This was not the tall man that she had seen before but a different man, small with charred, cracked, oozing skin, and eyes that were completely black. He shuffled when he walked, his movements appeared out of sync with the rest of the world. He smiled a wide grin of crooked, yellow teeth when he realized Cheryl could see him. "I knew you would come." His voice was like a river of nails.

Cheryl's heart pounded in her chest. She reached out and grabbed hold of Adam's arm, squeezing for comfort.

"What is it? What do you see?" he asked, his voice low.

"There's something there?" Janet looked wide-eyed in the direction that Cheryl was looking.

Cheryl didn't hear anything Adam or Janet said. She was locked in a world where they no longer existed. Only this man and his dark, soulless eyes occupied this space. She watched him, mesmerized by his movements. He took one step forward and then another, grinning a wide, crooked smile that opened even more fissures on his face. Then he spoke, "We almost have your friend. Once he says the words, the door will open all the way, and there'll be nothing you can do. He's getting close. He might say them any minute."

He nodded toward Adam, and Cheryl's surroundings came back into focus. They weren't alone in a void. They were in Janet's kitchen.

Cheryl turned to look at Adam, who was standing just a little bit behind her, and she saw his lips moving even though he wasn't saying a word. "Stop it, Adam! You have to stop it. If you say those words, you'll open the door." She pulled at his arm to get him to look at her.

Adam clamped his mouth shut. "Is someone there? Who do you see?"

"What door?" Janet asked, her words thick with panic.

The ghost flickered, his edges blurring and melting into the air around him. He faded and then came back more defined than he was before.

Janet stepped forward, placing her hand on Cheryl's shoulder. "That's him. That's the man I saw earlier today." She pointed at the man who spun in a circle on his heels, and when he came to a stop facing them, tipped an imaginary hat and gave a slight bow. Janet gripped Cheryl's shoulder a bit harder. Cheryl paid close attention to the man and tried to ignore the increasing pressure on her shoulder.

"What do you want?" she asked him.

He grinned and began to dance—shuffle tap, shuffle tap. He held his arms out at his side. "I want what I want, and that's all you need to know." His raspy voice grated through the air.

"But what do you want?" Cheryl stepped forward, wriggling her shoulder to loosen it from Janet's grip. She was certain she would have a bruise there tomorrow. "Why are you here? If we talk, maybe I can help you."

He stopped dancing and laughed, throwing his head back. "Who says I need your help?" He tapped his toe on the floor, took a step to the side, and then dragged his opposite foot across the tile floor. "I just need to dance a little longer, and I'll get what I want."

Cheryl was so busy paying attention to him that she didn't even notice Adam's mouth moving again. This time as the man danced, words began to spill out of Adam. Long words from an ancient language no one spoke anymore. Sharp and dangerous words spilled over his lips into the room.

"Adam, don't!" She was too late. He'd already finished the phrase. The ghost laughed, and then he ran at them all as fast as he could. His feet tapping on the tile as he ran straight into Adam and disappeared. Cheryl knew he wasn't gone because Adam turned and looked at her with the same sneer the ghost wore.

Chapter 17

The more the man danced, the less control Adam had over himself. He'd managed not to say the words all this time. It was hard, but it was doable partially because the syllables and sounds the book demanded him to say meant nothing to him. They got stuck on his tongue. Then the ghost danced, and that resistance began to go away. The more he danced, the more the words pressed into him. Demanding to be spoken, they pushed their way out of him, rolling off his tongue. His vocal cords squeezed and contracted, forcing out sound. It was as if he had no control anymore, and his body had become connected to something other than his mind. His body was connected to the skeletal man's feet. His voice followed the rhythm of his tap dancing. The words were sticky and sharp, but they came from his mouth more easily. He couldn't stop the flow. And when the last word had left his lips, he knew what he had done was so terrible it might be beyond repair.

Then the ghost ran at him. Adam's natural instinct was to jump out of the way, but he couldn't move. His feet were stuck in place, and the ghost ran right into him. Adam braced himself for the impact, but there was no impact because the ghost did not collide with him but instead jumped into his body.

Immediately, Adam's consciousness was pushed down. He was aware but no longer in control. His body began to move. He was aware of that but could not control it. His legs were not his own. He couldn't stop himself when he felt his hands encircle Cheryl's neck. When he felt his fingers squeezing and squeezing, he could do nothing but watch.

***

He came at her so quickly that Cheryl had no idea what to do. He ran toward her with his arms outstretched, his mouth open in a sinister cackle as he clamped his hands around her neck and began to squeeze. Cheryl reached up and grabbed his forearms. He squeezed her throat so hard she could feel the cartilage giving way and her windpipe begin to give. She pushed her arms up through the center between his forearms and struck them, in an attempt to escape his grasp. He loosened his grip, but he didn't let go. Her mind raced, and her ears rang. The edges of her vision began to go dark. Was this how she was going to die?

All she could see was Adam's face twisted into a sinister grin. His eyes had gone completely black, just like the ghost's. Cheryl was struggling beneath him when she heard a zap, and Adam dropped to the floor. His body arched in pain. Behind him, Janet held a taser.

"I couldn't just stand there and let him kill you." She looked into Cheryl's eyes. "I feel terrible about doing that to him. He's been so helpful but—"

"He's not Adam. He's someone else." She rubbed the sore spot on her throat and looked around the kitchen. "Do you have anything we can tie him up with?"

Janet ran out of the room and came back within seconds with a bundle of white nylon rope. They worked together, tying his hands behind his back and his feet together. He breathed heavily and had a stunned look in his eyes.

"I hope I didn't hurt him too bad. I only bought this thing yesterday and haven't had a chance to try it out yet." Janet wrapped a length of rope around his ankles.

Cheryl was too busy trying to figure out what to do next to answer. Just as she tied the last knot around his wrist, he came to. He twisted his head to the side and opened his mouth, letting out a roar.

"What do you think you're doing?" he said in a voice that was no longer Adam's.

Cheryl ignored him and tied the last knot. Janet stood by the doorway of the kitchen, looking down at him.

"What's going on back there?"

They heard Yvette's footsteps coming up the hall.

"Go distract her. I don't want her to see this. Tell her everything's okay," Cheryl whispered to Janet, who put the taser on the table and immediately left the room. Cheryl heard her telling Yvette that everything was fine.

Adam wriggled around on the floor. "Tying me up won't stop what is bound to happen."

"I know, but it will give me time."

Janet came back into the room looking out of breath. She wiped the sweat from her forehead. "I don't think she believed me, but she went back to the room with Frank. What do we do now?"

What do we do now? That was the question, and Cheryl didn't know the answer. "Who are you?"

He rolled over onto his side so he could look at her more easily. His black eyes reflected everything that he saw back at her. "We out number you. On the other side, we wait, looking for the opportunity to cross over into this side so we can affect your life. It's all good fun and games that could eventually become more." His mouth twisted unnaturally as he talked. "There are too many of us. You can't stop us."

"Where are the others?" She remembered the spiral of beings over Frank's bed and wondered if those thousands and thousands of beings were perched at the gate waiting for their chance to crossover like this one had.

"We're coming soon."

Cheryl needed to keep him talking; she needed answers. "When?"

He looked her over as if appraising her before answering. "Wouldn't you like to know? We like surprises."

Cheryl thought of the book that she had made Adam leave in the car and wondered if the answer was somewhere in there.

The room began to shake. At first, she thought it was the work of the ghost inside Adam, but when she looked down, she saw fear in his eyes. She wondered if it was him or Adam she saw in that moment. "Adam?"

He didn't answer. Instead, his gaze danced around the room as if looking for something. So Cheryl looked around the room too and when her eyes fell upon what he must have seen, she wasn't overcome with fear, she felt a sense of relief.

The tall, pale ghost she'd seen in the room with Frank stood hunched over in the doorway. He walked toward Adam, holding one hand out in front of him as if telling someone to stop. Cheryl watched him with wide eyes. Reaching out, he seemed to stick his hand inside Adam's throat, his fingers vanishing in Adam's flesh. He strained and yanked his arm back, pulling out the ghost who had jumped into Adam.

"Be gone!" the tall ghost yelled before unleashing a flurry

of ancient-sounding words similar to the ones Adam had spoken earlier.

The very air seemed to protest. The space around them squeezed and contracted. The floor bucked. Cheryl fell, her knees landing painfully on the hard tile.

The tall man held the other ghost by his collar in the air, his feet dangling just over Adam's now limp body. Cheryl leaned over him and tried to determine if he was breathing as the room shook around them.

"What's happening?" Janet cried out.

Cheryl looked over to see Janet gripping the kitchen table, her eyes wide with fear. "Don't worry. I've—" Before she could finish the sentence, she fell to the ground in a heap.

**

Adam opened his eyes to find himself in complete darkness. Everything around him was the deepest black. He lay on his back on the floor, which was as smooth as glass. His hands rested on the cold surface next to his legs. All around him was silence and stillness. He sat up, not knowing where he was. The last thing he remembered was that he was in Janet's kitchen and that strange charred-looking ghost in the grimy suit had run at him. There was a struggle, not a physical one, but something internal as if struggling for control. The details of what had happened ran together. First, he was standing in the kitchen, then everything around him was falling away, and now he was here. It all happened too quickly to process.

In the darkness, he found his way to his feet. Cold air settled around him.

"Hello?" he called into the void. "Is anyone here?"

His voice echoing back was the only answer he heard. He

stood still for a moment, wondering what to do next and hoping he wouldn't be here forever. The darkness was so thick that it seemed to grip him. Tentatively, he slid his foot along the smooth, hard ground, testing to make sure there was actually something there to support him before stepping forward. It didn't matter which direction he went because all directions led into more darkness. He eased himself forward cautiously, keenly aware that the floor could drop out from under him. He could be approaching a cliff and not even know it. He eased himself forward, with his arms outstretched in front of him, hoping to hear or see something besides silent darkness.

The sound started as a whisper tickling his eardrums. Then it grew into a rush, like an incoming wave. Suddenly something was brushing by him, like a million wings flitting against his skin. Fear gripped his insides, but he stayed completely still, hoping whatever was rushing past him would do so without injuring him. Then it began to lift him into the air. His feet left the floor. His arms flailing out to his side, he tried to anchor himself to something, but there was nothing to grab. Whatever was rushing past him wasn't solid. It tickled the bare skin of his arms and scurried across his palms. His body stiffened as he was raised further and further from the ground. Then there was a whoosh, and he saw Janet's kitchen again. The scene rushed toward him. He was completely out of control. As he was flung into reality, he saw the charred-looking ghost. His mouth was open in a scream. His face twisted with anger. The world seemed to crack as Adam landed with a thud back into his body. Dizzy and disoriented, he looked around and just in time to see the tall ghost step into Cheryl, but when he tried to reach out to help her, he found his hands were tied behind his back.

**

Cheryl's whole body tensed. She knew what was going to happen, but she never got used to it. Her vision went fuzzy, and her eyes clouded as she dropped into the life of someone else.

Chapter 18

Armand found the book that would eventually destroy his life in an alley on his way home from work. At first, he thought he was lucky when he spotted it lying on the ground next to the dumpster. He loved books and couldn't resist rescuing this one from the landfill. As soon as he picked up the little book, it became his. Its dark blue cover was blank. Scuff marks on the edges and the discolored spots hinted at it being well-loved at one time. Armand turned the book over in his hand. The spine and back cover were also blank. Standing in the alley next to the dumpster at six thirty in the evening as the sun sank in the sky, Armand opened the book for the first time. There was no title page, just a silly rhyme inviting him to solve the puzzles inside.

This was an invitation Armand could not refuse. For all of his thirty-three years, he was a loner, substituting the companionship of books for friends. There was a time when he would've blamed his friendlessness on his height. A pituitary tumor that wasn't discovered until he was well into adolescence had allowed him to grow just over seven feet tall before he was fifteen. While many would think of being tall as a desirable characteristic, it didn't help a shy teenager who only wanted to be liked. He was all gangly arms and legs, and he stayed that way, having never quite grown into his height.

With the long weekend coming, Armand thought this book would make a perfect companion. As he walked away, holding it in his hand, he found himself looking over his shoulder, constantly afraid that someone might come up to him and claim ownership of it. Once he had gotten his hands on it, it felt like the most important object in the world. He went from not knowing it existed at all to needing to have it. It seemed to hum against his fingertips as he held it like a living, breathing being.

He rushed home, holding the book against his chest as if protecting it. His apartment was only a few blocks away, but it felt like miles. When he finally got inside, he closed the door and put the chain on.

Armand sat at the table in his kitchen with the book still pressed against his chest. He took a few deep breaths before laying it down. Gingerly, he flipped it open. The smooth, yellowing pages felt like they could break apart so easily. He scanned the contents, most of which were written in a language he had never seen before. Squiggles and lines all sat on each other in tight neat columns. He ran his fingers along the writing, feeling the indentation of the print on the page, and wondered what it could all mean. This book compelled him more than any other had before. Now that he'd looked at those pages, he would never be rid of it. He sat, running his hands along the pages until his fingertips tingled. He didn't need to read the words because the essence of what it had to say seemed to seep up through the paper into his skin.

Armand was a simple man with simple thoughts and simple desires. Maybe it was that simplicity that allowed him to get caught up in the web of the book so quickly. Once he started to look at the pages, they grabbed him, and he couldn't pull himself away. Though he couldn't understand the language he saw before him, the markings were hypnotic. They pulled him and left him constantly desiring more. The sun sank in the sky, and Armand continued to sit looking at the pages in the book, his eyes aching. His legs cramped. His feet fell asleep. His stomach rumbled with hunger, but he remained seated on the hard wooden chair at the table with his eyes turned downward, hoping to find the mysteries of the world in the pages of the book. He didn't realize the answers he felt the book might reveal were the type no human should ever know.

Some people are more impressionable than others, and ever since he was a small child, Armand knew he was one of those people. His world was full of longing; every suggestion of what he needed coiled its way around his heart, making him want for things. The results of that wanting piled up all around him in his tiny one-bedroom apartment. Tools he never used, clothing that didn't even fit him, electric blankets and collectible coins, and exercise equipment that promised to give him the perfect body surrounded him in precarious piles always threatening to topple over. When he did walk around his apartment, ducking through doorways because of his height, he had to be careful to avoid the piles. Once he opened the book, all the ducking and weaving, turning and twisting stopped. The book was all he saw. It was all he needed. It was all that existed. The mess his life had been disappeared.

When he did sleep, sitting at the kitchen table with his forehead resting on his hands, he dreamed of the book. He didn't answer the phone. He didn't answer the door. He grew thinner and thinner as he stared at the book until finally, the words on the pages unraveled in his head, revealing their meaning. The mystery was becoming clear to him. The markings on the page morphed into syllables, the syllables into words, the words into sounds that he could speak. They repeated themselves again and again in rhythm, asking to roll from his tongue and cross his lips. They begged to be spoken aloud. The words slithered from his mouth and curled through the air, wrapping themselves around every object in the room, opening up another dimension.

Armand knew from the beginning that he was not like everyone else. That much was obvious. In these moments, he realized that it wasn't that he was not as good as everyone else, but quite the opposite. He was better. He was more. His height was evidence of that.

His luck finding this book was evidence of that....

No.

It wasn't luck. It was destiny.

And it pointed to something important about his true nature. Armand was special in a way no one in this world could comprehend.

The words were warm water rolling over him, washing away what his life once was and reinventing him. The words were his rebirth into what he always secretly knew himself to be. As he spoke them aloud, they opened up his mind.

Armand stood from the chair he'd occupied, and the blood rushed into his legs. His muscles cried out from the shock of movement, but he was able to ignore the pain because he was pursuing something much bigger than the physical world. He stood with his arms outstretched. As he spoke the words again, a swirl of darkness like the deepest black hole opened over his head. A horde of skeletal beings rushed into his kitchen. Pale skin stretched taut over sharp bones. Their sickly bodies pressed in around him. Their mouths opened, and they chanted the words with him, releasing a giant noise into his tiny apartment.

The air roiled with malice. The sharp teeth of evil sank into him. Armand continued to chant, his arms outstretched, his knuckles pounding on the ceiling until they bled, leaving streaks of red on the white plaster. His throat strained, and his eyes hurt, but the demons egged him on. This was only the beginning. They needed him to say more to open the door all the way.

The noise was so loud that he didn't hear the knocking on his door. He didn't hear the phone ring. He didn't hear the yelling outside or the sirens of the approaching police car. He was only aware of the words giving him new life.

First, they knocked. Then they pounded. Then they broke the door down. Police, dressed in their black uniforms, charged into his apartment with their guns drawn. "You can't let them stop you," one of the demons whispered in his ears. "Then you'll never know our secrets."

Armand looked into its empty black eyes and knew it was right. He couldn't let anyone stop what he was doing because he was saving the world.

He turned to face the police rushing through his living room. Roaring, he launched himself at them. He never heard the gunshots but felt them like hot pokers searing his flesh. He left his body that day. He watched as his broken flesh was zipped into a body bag. That's when he realized what he'd done.

The demons lingered in his apartment around the half open hole as if waiting for something, so Armand stayed too. He wanted to see what they were doing.

While they waited, Armand studied the book that still was open on the table. He stood over it, studying the open page for days and weeks as the demons swirled impatiently around him doing their best to influence him, but without his flesh they could not latch onto him.

They were in limbo waiting for the hole to open all the way so they could walk freely in this world, but with no mortal to complete the spell they were stuck. Unencumbered by his body, Armand could now see the evil inside the demons. He knew he needed to send them back to where they came from before it was too late.

After hours of study, he learned the secret. It was so easy. To close the door he had to do the exact opposite of what he did to open it.

When Armand discovered the secret, he reveled in returning the demons to the darkest depths that they'd come from. Once his work was done, he could not leave the book. Something that had influenced him so completely would eventually influence someone new, and he had to be there to undo any harm it might cause.

Chapter 19

When Cheryl opened her eyes, she was on the floor.

"Are you okay?" Adam struggled against the rope binding his wrists on the floor beside her.

She nodded. "Are you?" The last thing she remembered was the skeletal man diving into him.

"I'd be even better if you untied me."

She barely remembered tying him up in the first place. She untied his wrists and ankles as quickly as she could as the house shook around them. Dishes and glasses crashed to the floor, sending sharp shards spraying around them. Janet crawled around sobbing, her hands and knees bloodied from the splinters of glass littering the tile.

The door to the other side was opening. Cheryl knew it and couldn't let it happen.

"We have to stop this," she said, as Adam rubbed the red marks the rope left on his wrists. Unsteady, she clambered to her feet and hurried to the door, unsure of what she would do once she discovered the source of the commotion. The house bucked violently, forcing her to hold onto the wall to stay upright. She made her way to Frank's room. The door was closed. She tried the doorknob only to find it locked. Twisting the knob, she pounded on the door. "Yvette, let me in."

No one answered.

"Is everything okay in there? Let me in." Her palm thudded against the solid wood of the door again and again.

Still, no one answered.

She heard gargling and looked to her left to see thick black goo oozing down the staircase.

Certain Yvette wasn't coming to open the door, she began to ram her shoulder into the door to force it open. Her shoulder met the door with force again and again, but the door was too strong.

Her shoulder ached by the time Adam was next to her, ramming into the door too. Finally, it popped open, revealing Yvette sitting in the chair next to Frank's bed wearing a blank expression. Frank was sitting up in bed chanting, the ancient book lay open in his lap.

"How did he get the book?" Cheryl asked. She specifically remembered him leaving it in the passenger seat of his car.

"I have no idea." Adam was already rushing into the room. Cheryl followed close behind.

A spiral of blackness opened over Frank's bed. Skeletal beings materialized and surrounded them, blocking their path. They hissed, baring long pointed teeth dripping with thick ropes of saliva. They yelled so loud Cheryl could not think. Cheryl gripped Adam's arm to keep herself grounded in reality as they pushed through the creatures to get to Frank.

Frank's eyes were shiny black mirrors. His face had transformed into something expressionless and robotic. Cheryl looked at him with fear swelling in her chest. Before she could do anything, Adam reached out and snatched the book from Frank's hands. In a flash, his eyes returned to normal, and confusion clouded his expression. Bewildered, he stared at the two of them like he was surprised to see them suddenly in front of him. Adam snapped the book closed, and the skeletal demons vanished.

Yvette blinked. "What happened?"

Janet, with dark red stains on the knees of her khaki slacks, stumbled through the door. She gripped the doorjamb leaving a smear of blood on the wall as she looked into the room, her eyes wide with horror. "Did you stop it?" Childlike fear loomed in her eyes.

"For now," Adam said.

Cheryl looked at him and noticed his lips moving again. She reached over and took the book from him. "I think I should hold onto that." She turned her attention to Janet. "We've done what can for the moment, but it's not over yet." Cheryl knew they could be stopped. Armand had showed her that. They only needed to figure out exactly what they needed Frank to say. She looked over at Adam and noticed he was moving his lips. The skeletal beings surrounded him, encouraging him to speak. "Adam, what are you doing? Stop doing that."

"What?" he asked.

"Moving your mouth like that. You can't say anything from the book. Do you understand?"

He nodded. "I know."

Then the tall ghost appeared next to him. Cheryl saw Armand and immediately felt relieved. He knew what to do. That's why he was here. Armand bent down and began to whisper in Adam's ear. Adam closed his eyes and pressed his lips together, struggling not to speak.

"Armand," Cheryl said. "Do you know how to fix this?"

He stood at his full height, pulling back his shoulders. He blinked slowly and nodded once.

"Adam, there's a ghost here. Can you see him?"

Adam looked around the room. "No, but I think I can feel him."

"There's a ghost here now?" Yvette's voice shook with fear. She rubbed the gold cross around her neck between her thumb and forefinger, her gaze darting around the room.

"Go away!" Janet yelled into the room. "Leave us alone."

"He's here to help you." Cheryl held a hand out to her, telling her to calm down. "He knows how to stop all of this because he experienced the same thing when he was alive." She looked at the tall ghost who smiled back at her. Then he bent over and began whispering in Adam's ear again. "Adam, repeat what he's telling you."

Cheryl couldn't hear what Armand said. As his mouth moved, Adam's mouth moved too until eventually, they spoke in unison. The words appeared to rewind time. The skeletal demons stretched and bent, their feet leaving the ground as they were sucked back up into the hole in the ceiling. Everything that had fallen to the floor in the violent shaking only a few moments previously returned to their shelves. A great sound came from the kitchen as all the glass shards drew themselves together again reforming plates, glasses, and vases. The goo that had flowed down the stairs slithered back up, leaving no trace of slime as it went.

Adam continued to chant, and Cheryl heard footsteps. The charred man came down the steps like a spider, his back arched and his body twisted. When he got to the bottom of the stairs, his bones crunched and cracked as he twisted his body around and stood.

Janet let out a yelp. "Make it stop."

Cheryl ignored her pleas. She was watching the charred man in the tattered suit. What would he do next? Not fazed by his presence, Adam continued to chant.

Shuffle, tap. Shuffle, tap. He danced right through the wall into the room with them. "Do you really think you can stop me with your sorry little chant. Put some feeling into it," he taunted.

Armand and Adam continued to speak. Their voices rose until their chanting filled the room. Adam threw his head back, his eyes rolling in their sockets, revealing only the white part of his eyes. He raised his hands in the air as if calling to a divine being to give him strength. Armand stood upright too, his head nearly touching the ceiling. He walked over to Frank and whispered in his ear. Frank looked at Janet, his eyes wide with fear.

"It's okay," Cheryl said. "Repeat the words you hear. It's the only way to undo this."

"No, it isn't." The charred man danced over to Frank's bedside too. Shuffle, tap. Shuffle, tap.

Frank turned and looked at him and Cheryl realized he could see him.

"Don't listen to him." Cheryl rushed over to Frank's bedside too. "He's the one that's caused all of this. We need him to go away. Listen to him." Cheryl pointed at Armand, hoping Frank could see him too.

Frank didn't look there though. He looked past everyone to his wife. Janet stood in the doorway with tears running down her face. "Please make it all stop. I need it to stop, Frank."

A tear slipped down Frank's face. He glanced at Cheryl and then he opened his mouth and began to speak. Armand, Frank, and Adam chanted in unison. Their voices rising above every sound in the house. The charred man groaned and fell to his knees, his hands over his ears.

Words, guttural and sharp, sliced through the air. Just when Cheryl was sure it was all over. The charred man struggled to his feet. He opened his mouth to speak, and the words seemed to come out in reverse. He tried to speak again and still only produced a garble of sounds.

The book vibrated in Cheryl's hand. Startled, she dropped it to the floor. It opened on its own and a bright yellow light shot out from the pages. The charred man let out a scream before being sucked into the light. The book snapped shut.

Adam, Frank, and Armand all stopped chanting. Frank and Adam looked at each other, relieved.

Cheryl watched as Armand seemed to melt away. "It's over for now," he said in his deep hollow voice. Slowly he vanished, leaving only the living in the room.

Chapter 20

"Do you think everything's out of their house?" Adam asked as he drove the car slowly down the narrow suburban street. They'd gone from room to room checking the house for signs of entities before they left.

"Definitely." Cheryl was sure of very few things in her life, but she was sure of that. She had listened with every part of her as she walked around the house. Once she was certain no trace of supernatural activity remained, she had burned some sage to get rid of the last vestiges of any evil lurking there.

The book that started this whole mess was laying on the backseat of the car. Cheryl twisted around to look at it there. It seemed so innocuous. "What should we do with that?"

Adam shrugged. He turned the wheel of the car, and they joined the traffic on the main road. "I was thinking of holding onto it."

Cheryl gaped at him. "Are you crazy? You can't hold onto it. I saw the way it got its claws into you. You can't risk that happening again." She scowled at him. "That's probably why you want to keep it. The book's making you say that. How do you know you're strong enough not to call up whatever demon that was again?"

"So you don't have faith in me?" He smirked. The twinkle in his eye told her that he was joking.

"That's not funny." She smacked his arm. "We seriously have to get rid of it." She looked out the window. She was exhausted.

"We're going to burn it," he said. He pulled into a gas station. "But first we need some book burning supplies." He got out of the car. "Do you need anything?"

She shook her head. "Nope. I'll just wait here."

If she didn't think about her finances, she could imagine her life was finally coming together, but that daydream was quickly shattered by the sound of her phone buzzing in her bag. She didn't even bother to check it anymore. She'd made the mistake of opening one of the letters from the credit card company that morning, and it said something about taking her to court. She hoped they couldn't do that. Maybe that's what it meant when she pulled the Tower card the other day. It felt like her financial life was already burning to the ground, but she knew things could get a lot worse.

Adam walked back from the gas station with a bag dangling from his fingertips. "I got lighter fluid and matches." He got into the car.

"We're ready for a book barbecue." The idea of burning the book made her feel uneasy too, but they had to get rid of it.

His phone beeped, and he pulled it from his pocket.

"Who is it?" she asked, hoping it wasn't Janet texting to tell them things were getting weird in their house again.

"My sister. I keep forgetting to call her. Remind me to do it when we're done with all this." He put the car in reverse and backed out of their space. They didn't turn to go downtown like they normally would have. Instead, he turned to get on the highway.

"Where are we going?" Cheryl watched the scenery whiz by them.

"I want to burn it away from people's houses just in case."

"In case, what?" she asked.

Adam shrugged. "I don't know, but we shouldn't put anyone in harm's way. I have no idea what's going to happen when we set that thing on fire."

He was right. Cheryl had never burned a magical book before. She didn't even know if it was possible. "Where can we go? Tons of people live here. I don't think there's any place where there isn't a house." She looked out the window. The passing trees were only a thin strip of greenery to shield the neighborhoods from the highway.

"Don't worry. I have an idea."

They went south, crossing the Skyway Bridge. Cheryl looked out at the expanse of water around them, so blue and beautiful. "There's so much darkness in the world." She looked down at the water as she spoke, breaking their silence.

"There is a lot of good too. Look at Janet and Frank and all of the people we've met."

"I know. There are wonderful people out there, but I'm not talking about people. I never realized that there's all this evil bubbling just beneath the surface of everything, trying desperately to get out. I walked around for so long, only seeing the surface and having no idea what was underneath." She pressed her lips together and thought for a moment. She wasn't quite sure what she was trying to say. "I haven't had it easy in life. My family wasn't that great, and then there was Mark." She shook her head. "You know how things have been. It's hard to be optimistic, but I try. You know I've tried my best to look on the bright side and keep going. I've always thought there was something better out there for me, even when it was hard, and it seemed like I'd never find it. These days after seeing what we've seen, I'm a lot less optimistic." She looked over at him. He concentrated on the road. She could tell by the way his forehead creased that what she was saying stressed him. "In a way, I feel like all of this has ruined me." She snorted. "That's not right. I guess I was already ruined in a way."

"You're not ruined." Adam reached over and turned off the radio that had been playing quietly ever since they'd been in the car. "I'm not going to pretend it's not hard knowing there are other worlds parallel to our own, and the things that live in those other worlds aren't all sunshine and sausages."

Cheryl laughed. "Sunshine and sausages?"

"That's something my sister always says. Knowing about what's really going on is a big responsibility. It means we have to do more. Even though it's not exactly easy, I wouldn't trade it for the world. I feel like this is what I was meant to do, don't you?" He glanced over at her.

She bit her bottom lip and furrowed her brow before giving a reluctant nod. "Well, I guess I do. It's good to have a purpose in life because I was kind of roaming around without one before, but I'm tired of feeling scared. I was terrified when I was married to Mark. I came here hoping to put all the fear behind me, but now I have something new to be afraid of."

"Stop being afraid, then. Yes, we do face some pretty horrifying things, but every single time we've come out on top. Your walking around being afraid of what could be when nothing's happening doesn't help anyone. Deal with the fear when it's necessary, but in your daily life, there's no reason to be afraid. Life has gotten better for me since all of this."

"How so?"

"I've got a purpose. I've got direction. I'm helping good

people live better lives. It's meant so much more than just getting rid of a computer virus." The trees were thick all around them, and Adam pulled off the highway onto the shoulder.

"What are we doing?"

"If we're going to burn a book, this is as good a place as any to do it." Adam reached into the backseat and grabbed hold of it. He jolted when his fingertips touched its front cover, pausing for a moment before picking it up.

"Are you okay?" Cheryl put her hand on his arm.

He didn't answer right away. "Yeah, I'm totally fine."

She didn't like the way he shook his head when he said that. "Are you sure?" She narrowed her eyes at him.

"Yes. I'm sure." With the book in hand, he got out of the car and walked into the woods. Cheryl followed close behind him.

***

Adam was not fine, but he didn't want Cheryl to know. What had to be done had to be done, no matter how he felt. The book knew their intention though, and when he reached for it in the backseat, it shocked him. He winced but kept his hand on the book. Whatever this was, he was determined to defeat it. Taking it from the back seat, he got out of the car and walked into the woods with Cheryl close behind him. The lighter fluid and matches in the shopping bag he carried had an ominous weight to them.

"This is crazy. Where are we going?" She was close on his heels as they walked through the underbrush into the forest.

Adam could see how this would seem strange to her or anyone for that matter. He wanted to explain what he was doing, but he had to focus so the book wouldn't completely take him over. It took everything in his power to continue walking forward. His muscles wanted to seize up. He ached all over but pressed on, walking into the woods. The words the book had told him before came back to his mind. They repeated and repeated again and again, compelling him to speak, but he had to ignore it. Everything was dependent on him ignoring it. Silently he walked forward. He focused on their footsteps and the sound of the branches breaking underfoot.

"Adam, you're scaring me. Where are we going?" Cheryl asked again. She ran a little, holding her skirt up so it wouldn't get caught in the underbrush. When she was next to him, she grabbed hold of his arm, but he yanked it away.

"I'm sorry." He spoke in a whisper. "It's the book. I have to focus."

"You're not going to do anything bad, are you?" She spoke as quietly as he did now. "I mean, you're not going to unleash the fires of Hell or something, are you?" Her voice rose at the end of that sentence.

Adam shook his head because that's all he could do. They walked slowly through the trees. He knew exactly where he was going. This was where he was from and where he was going was his hangout as a teenager. It didn't take long for them to get to the clearing. It was only a ten-minute walk into the trees.

When they got to the clearing, an oblong patch of grass lay before them, yellowing from the dry weather. Adam had spent so much time in this field as a teenager with his friends. Back then, he thought of this place as a refuge from adults. Not even his sister knew about it. From the beer cans scattered around, he could tell this was still a spot the teenagers in the area used. A rusty metal drum sat in the middle of the field just like he remembered. A few logs sat around it for people to use to sit on when they had a fire going. Adam gritted his teeth and walked straight through the clearing to the drum. This was the fastest he had moved since they got out of the car. When he got to the drum he dropped the grocery bag, letting it fall into the brittle grass.

"Are you okay?" Cheryl reached down and picked up the bag and pulled out the lighter fluid and matches. "So, this is where we burn the key to opening the gates of Hell." She looked over at him, but he continued to stare blankly at the metal drum before them.

The voices filled his head now, a steady rhythmic chant. The words were demanding to be spoken, but he knew he couldn't say them. It was too hard to focus. He was unclear why he was here anymore. He looked over at her, and she watched him with fear in her eyes.

"Are you okay?" she repeated.

Adam wanted to say no. He should have said no. Instead, he nodded. He looked down at the book in his hand. The dingy blue cover had been in this world for so long. Now he was going to try to destroy it. It seemed wrong. It wasn't what he should do, was it?

He flipped it open, wanting to look at the pages one last time. He ran his fingers along the smooth paper. Maybe he could say just a few of the words just this one time before he destroyed it forever. He opened his mouth to speak; the first syllable came out. And then another. And then...

**

When Adam started reading from the book, Cheryl couldn't believe what she was hearing. She acted before she thought, snatching the book from him and throwing it into the metal drum. "What do you think you're doing?" Anger surged through her even though she knew she shouldn't be angry with him. It wasn't his fault. The book was controlling him.

As soon as it left his hands, he snapped out of his trance. He looked around as if he was confused and didn't remember walking out into this field. She wanted to help him, but she knew the only way to do that was to get rid of that stupid book. Hastily, she opened the lighter fluid and aimed it into the barrel to spray it on the book. She looked back at Adam to see if he would stop her, but he watched her blankly.

She ran the red-tipped match along the side of the box, two, three, four times before it finally lit. She dropped the match inside. Blue flames shot out of the barrel with a whoosh, and the black smoke rose into the sky.

"I can't believe I'm actually burning a book." Cheryl looked around, expecting something terrible to happen. She expected the jaws of Hell to open one last time to try swallow them up.

Adam said nothing. He stood watching the flame. They both backed away because the heat was so great.

"I always associated book burning with fringe religious sects and lunatic politicians. And now here I am burning what might've been the oldest book in the world. It feels wrong even though I know it's the right thing to do." She tried to sound lighthearted, but underneath there was a sadness in what she was doing. Yes, she was destroying the key to open the door to Hell, but it felt like she was also destroying something very important, a part of history.

"I know what you mean." He stuck his hands in his pockets as they watched the flames dance. "Hopefully, this will really stop it. I don't feel it anymore."

"What do you mean hopefully? I thought we were doing this because you knew something I didn't."

"I thought burning it was your idea."

Cheryl shook her head.

"Well, no matter whose idea it was, I hope it works," he said.

Cheryl hoped it work too, but now she had her doubts.

They stood in the field watching the flame with the sun blazing down on them. When the fire finally burned out, they both walked up to the edge of the barrel together and peered in. All that was left of the book was a pile of white ash at the bottom of the barrel.

Cheryl looked at Adam. "Did it work?" she asked.

He shrugged. "I guess we'll find out."

Chapter 21

"What's that?" Cheryl pointed through the windshield at the column of smoke billowing in the air as they turned onto Central Avenue.

"It looks like there's a fire." Adam leaned back in his seat and closed his eyes. Burning the book had taken everything out of him.

Cheryl gripped the steering wheel a little too tightly as she drove toward the smoke. She'd always hated driving other people's cars, but Adam had been so out of it that there was no way she'd let him drive.

She didn't realize the plume of smoke was coming from her building until she rounded the corner to see the street blocked off and firetrucks parked haphazardly out front.

Her eyes widened as flames shot from the windows. "Beau!" she yelled, jumping out of the car. She left it in the middle of the street and ran toward the building. Beau had been with her ever since she'd moved to St. Pete. She'd found him as a stray huddled against the wall in an alley in a downpour. It seemed like a sign. She'd taken him home that evening because she finally had a home she could take someone to. Ever since then, he'd been her companion. He was always there when times were rough. He'd sit in her lap purring and rub his cheek against her when she cried. She wasn't ready to be without him—not yet.

"Ma'am, you can't go beyond this point." A police officer held his hand up in the universal sign to stop.

"I live there. That's my neighbor." She pointed at Mr. Duncan who was stood next to a fire truck with Daisy running around in circles at his feet.

She ran toward him before the police officer could say anything else. "Mr. Duncan!"

He spun around, looking for the person calling his name.

A pane of glass shattered somewhere. The firefighters were telling everyone to get back. The world around her moved at a hyperaccelerated pace, but Cheryl felt like she was stuck in mud.

"It'll be okay. They're only things," Mr. Duncan said when she reached him. "We still have what matters." He looked down and for the first time she noticed he was carrying something. Beau's soft head poked out of his arms.

Tears erupted from Cheryl's eyes. "I didn't realize you had him. I thought he was dead."

Mr. Duncan happily handed the fat tabby cat over. She nuzzled his smooth and silky head. "Thank you." She wiped tears away from her face with a free hand. "But how did you get him out?"

"I didn't. He got himself out by jumping out the window. I just picked him up." Cheryl looked up at the building, where flames were still shooting out of the windows. She lived on the fourth floor and couldn't imagine Beau jumping that far and being okay. She held the cat in the air, his body arching around her hand, and looked him in the eyes. "Are you okay, Beau?" Then she pulled him into her again and squeezed him close. The cat only purred in her arms, and she knew instinctively that he would be okay.

Daisy jumped on her leg and barked a few times, and Cheryl bent down and patted the dog on the head.

"How did the fire start?"

Mr. Duncan shook his head. "I don't know. I heard someone say it started in an apartment on the second floor, but I have no idea what happened." They stood silently watching the dark smoke billowing into the sky. "Maybe I'll move to Miami," Mr. Duncan said casually.

Cheryl didn't understand how he could be so casual about something like this. Everything she had was gone now. Granted, she didn't have much, but she had worked hard for it. She had no idea how she was even supposed to deal with a loss like this.

"Such a shame to lose this building. It's been here so long." Mr. Duncan's voice pulled her out of her own panicked thoughts. "If this had happened even a week ago, I would've been devastated. It is terrible, but I know I don't have to be here to be close to Roy. It's all just stuff. That's what I keep telling myself at least."

"I don't know what I'm going to do." Cheryl couldn't feel anything anymore.

"We'll just have to take things one day at a time." He looked down at her purse. "At least you have your wallet." He patted the pockets of his Bermuda shorts. "I ran out without mine."

Cheryl felt a hand on her shoulder and turned around to see Adam. "They didn't want to let me through." He put his arm around her back and pulled her into him. "This is terrible. I'm so sorry."

"I've been through worse." Mr. Duncan gave Cheryl a knowing look before gazing across the crowd of people gawking at the scene. "I'm going to talk to Lucille." He pointed at the petite woman in a pale pink sweat suit with short gray hair. He started to walk away, but before he did, he turned back to Cheryl and said, "Thank you for what you told me before. It changed everything for me."

"You're welcome. I was glad I was able to help."

Mr. Duncan walked over to her. He held open his arms and gave her a hug. It was strange to hug this old man who had spent most of his time complaining about her, but something about it felt good too. The hug was awkward and when he pulled away from her, he held onto her shoulders. "You're out of the building and so is your cat. You're going to be okay." Then he turned around and made his way through the crowd to the woman in the sweat suit.

"He's right, you know. It's going to be okay." Adam squeezed her shoulder.

Cheryl wanted desperately to believe them, but she couldn't help but think of the Tower card Day had pulled for her earlier that week. This felt like the beginning of everything falling down around her.

***

Adam was headed home when he bumped into Sofia in the hallway. "Leaving so soon?" She smiled at him.

"Yeah. I was only in for a few hours today." The office was unusually noisy. A group of people stood in the corner talking loudly and laughing. A phone somewhere rang continually. Adam wondered if someone was going to answer it.

Sofia surveyed the scene. Then she raised an eyebrow at him. "Aren't you lucky."

"That I am." He was anxious to leave because he had a few updates he wanted to make to Suncoast Paranormal's website.

"Do you still have a girlfriend?" She pulled her long ponytail over her left shoulder, running her hand down the length of it.

"As a matter of fact, I do. She moved into my place a couple days ago." It was unfortunate that Cheryl's building had to burn down before she accepted his invitation to move into his condo. It'd only been two days and a lot of that time had been spent replacing things she had lost in the fire or at least trying to, but she seemed to be settling in well.

"Oh, so you're moving on to the next step. This might be the one." Her voice was a little higher than usual, and Adam wondered what that meant.

"Yeah, she might be the one." He had known that Cheryl was definitely the one for a long time, but he knew it was too soon to tell her that. She needed time.

Sofia looked him up and down as if appraising him. "Well, good for you. Or should I say good for her."

A firm hand landed on Adam's shoulder, and he turned around, startled.

"I'm glad I caught you before you left." Ethan stood before him, slightly out of breath. He looked at Sofia who stood watching him. "I need to talk to Adam alone." Before Adam or Sofia could say anything, Ethan grabbed his arm and dragged Adam up the hallway to his office.

Adam turned back to Sofia and held up his hand to gesture to her that he had no idea what this could possibly be about.

She smiled before spinning on her heels and returning to her desk.

Ethan shut the door to his office and stepped in close to Adam to talk. His voice was hushed as if getting ready to tell him a secret. "I really need you to come to my house and help me out with something. Things have gotten pretty out of hand there with my girls and my mother." Beads of sweat glistened on his forehead.

"What's going on?"

"I don't even know, man. It's gotten really strange over there. To be honest, it's making me nervous." He shook his head rapidly as he talked.

"Can you give me an example of what happened?" Ethan's attitude had shifted greatly. Adam could tell this was no longer about putting on a show to appease his family. This was something more.

Ethan glanced at the closed door. "This is going to sound nuts, but I swear on my father's grave that I was sitting in my living room last night and a kid that wasn't either of my girls came into the room, sat down in the middle of the floor, and started playing with a truck. My wife was out with the girls. My mother was out with her friends. I was at home by myself, and this kid comes in from out of nowhere. I'm thinking who on earth is this. So, I ask him, and he looks over at me and that's when I notice that he looks just like I did when I was a kid."

Now he really had Adam's attention. "You're kidding."

"I'm not done yet." Ethan held up a finger. "So, I say hey what's your name? And he didn't say anything. He gets up and runs back up the hallway to my daughter's bedroom. I follow him and when I get back there, there's no one there. I checked every place—under the beds, the closets, the bathroom. Nobody. Nothing. Nada. Zilch. I'm thinking I must be seeing things. I've been really tired recently, you know? But then I go back into the living room and the truck is still right there on the floor next to the coffee table. I go over to pick it up and realize it's the truck I used to play with when I was six years old. I turned it over and my name is written on the bottom in black marker just like I remember from when I was kid." He raised both eyebrows and lowered his chin at Adam like he was waiting for him to say something.

Adam started to speak, but before he could say anything Ethan started talking again.

"I thought, okay maybe I didn't see this kid. Maybe that was all a figment of my imagination or something, but I definitely have my old truck. So as my family members all came home, I asked everyone and nobody knew anything about it. My wife and girls said they'd never seen it before. My mother said she'd given it away to the kid up the street when I grew out of playing with it."

"That is strange. And nobody knew anything about it?"

"I just told you that." Ethan wiped the sweat from his forehead. "I don't know about that ghost stuff you're into, but do you think you can do something about what's going on in my house? It's not right. Something is definitely not right."

"We can take a look and see if it's anything we can do about it." Adam was overjoyed to have another case so quickly, but he was flummoxed by what Ethan had told him.

"Great. Can you come tomorrow night? I want to do this as soon as possible."

Adam wasn't sure about Cheryl's schedule, but if she had a reading he would go on his own. "Tomorrow night will work."

Relief washed over Ethan. "Thank you."

"I haven't done anything yet." Adam turned to leave.

"But knowing you'll check it out makes me feel better." He looked at his office door. "Sorry I ripped you away from your conversation with Sofia."

"Don't worry about it. I was just leaving."

As Adam left the office, he hoped they'd really be able to help Ethan. He had no idea that this case would ultimately force him even farther into parallel dimensions, forcing him and Cheryl to seek help in the most unlikely place.

Chapter 22

Adam's leather sofa creaked as Cheryl sat down. There was so much she would need to do to straighten out all that she had lost in the fire. First, she needed to get a landline hooked up so that she could continue to do her shifts on the Psychic Hotline. She thought about Roy and Mr. Duncan and how their chance to have a life together had been ripped away without warning. She didn't want to have regrets anymore. Even though her apartment burning down had pulled the rug out from under her, maybe it was for the best. If her place hadn't burned to the ground, she never would've moved in with Adam. It had only been a few days, but she liked living with him. She had been afraid of taking a chance on the guy, but she knew it was time to let that fear go. Holding onto it was only letting Mark continue to control her life.

She looked around at Adam's living room that was now her living room too. Black-and-white landscape pictures hung on the walls. Light poured in through the windows. She could easily see herself living here for a long time. The truth was that it would be so much easier to pick up the pieces of her life with someone else to help her. Even though she was reluctant to admit it, she had fallen in love with him. Sometimes everything had to fall apart for you to truly be able to put it all together again.

Tired, she stretched out her legs on the couch and closed her eyes for a few moments. She needed some peace so she could sort through all that had happened in the past few days.

Her eyes were closed when she felt her phone vibrating in her hand. It was Janet Tate. "Hello?"

"Is this Cheryl?" There was a lightness in Janet's voice that Cheryl had never heard before. "I know I'd been talking to Adam on the phone before, but your number is on the card too. I hope you don't mind."

"Of course I don't mind. My number is on the card for a reason. How are you?" She just realized they had forgotten to contact her after destroying the book.

"It's gone, isn't it? You got rid of it."

"Yes, we did."

"I can tell. Everything feels different here now." Cheryl heard footsteps. She heard a door creak as it opened. There was a muffled voice.

"I'm glad to hear it. We burned the book as soon as we left your house." She'd been thinking about that moment ever since it happened—the whoosh of the flame in the can. Was that fire connected to her apartment building burning down?

"They burned it," Janet said to someone else. "Frank's awake and more himself than I've seen him in a long time." Her voice trembled. "Thank you." She paused. "You've given me my Frank back."

"I'm glad to hear that." Knowing she could help Janet and Frank enjoy his last days almost made Cheryl forget that she'd just lost everything.

"It wouldn't have happened without you. I owe you so much more than you can imagine."

"We were only doing our jobs, but this call has made my day. Thank you for letting me know how you feel." This was exactly why she was so willing to face her fears and go into the haunted places that other people would run away from. Sometimes she witnessed so much sorrow and pain, but it was all worth it if she could help someone like this. Hearing the relief in Janet's voice on the phone and seeing the realization in Mr. Duncan's eyes when he found out his true love still thought of him brought her more joy than anything she'd ever done. These were the rewards for taking the hard road that she and Adam had chosen, and she was grateful for them. After she hung up from her call with Janet, she was still sitting on the couch thinking about that when the door opened.

Adam was on the phone when he walked into the apartment. "Yes, I got your text. I've just been so busy." He paused. "Okay, you're right, I forgot. I'm sorry. I am still freelancing on top of starting my own business, and"—he looked at Cheryl—"did I tell you that Cheryl's apartment building burned down?" He sat next to her. "Yeah, that was her building. So, she's living with me now." He leaned forward with his elbows on his knees and listened.

The person on the other end was speaking loudly, but Cheryl couldn't quite make out what she was saying.

Adam's face tensed as he listened. "She told you that?"

Then the person on the other end was talking again. This time her voice was faster and more urgent.

"When did that happen?"

The person spoke again.

"Why didn't you call me?" He got up and pulled his keys from his pocket. "Yeah, but everyone knows that you don't send a vague text that says, 'call me when you get a chance' if it's an emergency." He motioned to Cheryl to follow him to the door. "Yeah, we're coming right over." He hung up.

"What was that?"

"My sister. We have to go to her house now. There's something wrong with my niece." He yanked the door open and sprinted up the hallway forgetting to lock it behind him.

Cheryl fumbled with her new key to lock the door, before running after him along the hallway to set out on a new case.

ABOUT THE AUTHOR

Lovelyn Bettison writes stories about things that go bump in the night. She lives in St. Petersburg, Florida with her husband, son, and dog. She loves getting letters in the mail, Thai food, and having conversations with strangers in coffee shops. Find out more about her on her website: lovelynbettison.com.

MORE BOOKS BY LOVELYN BETTISON

SUNCOAST PARANORMAL

Monster in the House
Lady in the Lake
Girl in the Woods
Demon in the Mirror

ISLE OF GODS SERIES

The Vision
The Escape
The Memory
The Revenge (Coming Soon)

THE HAUNTING SERIES

The Haunting of Warren Manor (Coming Soon)

More Books by Lovelyn Bettison

UNCOMMON REALITIES SERIES

Perfect Family
The Box
Flying Lessons

STARLIGHT CAFE SERIES

The Barista
The Psychic
The Widow

SUNCOAST PARANORMAL

Woman in the Window
Lady in the Lake (Coming Soon)
Girl in the Woods (Coming Soon)

ISLE OF GODS SERIES

The Vision
The Escape
The Memory
The Revenge (Coming Soon)